CONFLICT & HONOR

a story by

MAY MOSS

iUniverse, Inc.
New York   Bloomington

Conflict & Honor

This is a work of fiction. All of the characters, names, incidents, organizations, and dialogue in this novel are either the products of the author's imagination or are used fictitiously.

iUniverse books may be ordered through booksellers or by contacting:

iUniverse
1663 Liberty Drive
Bloomington, IN 47403
www.iuniverse.com
1-800-Authors (1-800-288-4677)

ISBN: 978-0-595-50308-7 (pbk)
ISBN: 978-0-595-49813-0(cloth)
ISBN: 978-0-595-61458-5 (ebk)

Printed in the United States of America

Unending, never enough praise,
for JC, who loves me daily & unconditionally a moment at a time.

To my sweeties, Asha-Monique and Elijah D.-
without your love, life would have remained unbearable.
Cheryl "Pokemon Mom" thanks for your "show, not tell" input. Love does
many things, but it never fails

Contents

DRILL SERGEANT'S CREED

I am a Drill Sergeant.
I will assist each individual
in their efforts to become a
highly motivated, well disciplined,
physically and mentally fit soldier,
capable of defeating any enemy on
today's modern battlefield.
I will instill pride
in all I train.
Pride in self, in the Army,
and in country.
I will insist that each soldier
meet and maintain the Army standards
of military bearing and courtesy,
consistent with the highest traditions
of the US Army.
I will lead by example,
never requiring a Soldier to
attempt any task
I would not do myself.
But first, last and always,
I am an American Soldier.
Sworn to defend the constitution
of the United States against
all enemies, both foreign and domestic.
I am A Drill Sergeant
This Will Defend
the Creed of the United States Drill Sergeant

author unknown

in the beginning

Hurried footsteps touching every other stair startled Ginny. Afraid, she didn't turn to face the approaching sound. She inhaled, then released a short sigh, barely breathing, she waited to see who would appear, as she remembered her life two years ago.

It was her junior year in high school. Charlie, often told her, "We're pressed on the left by racism and pressed on the right by wanna-be black folks, setting up their own oppressive social class." She'd listen, closely to his ranting about how ignorant wanna-bes are, and their being too stupid to see how all black folks were receiving the same jive education in the same run down school, but instead of standing together, they wanted to separate themselves. "Wanna-bes think they're better off 'cause they got better jobs, more money, and live outside the hood. Yea, they may not live in the Lower End, but they need to recognize they are but a stone throw away living in its shadow," he'd passionately rage on as his fiery eyes smolder contemptuously, when he talked about how wanna-bes thought they were better than them. Whole-heartedly she supported Charlie's view. So much so, that earlier during the year she ran for school president with his help on a platform to unite the groups by one common cause, to have quality education in their school, regardless where anyone lived, because there was only one school that served 7th through 12th grade kids. It bothered Charlie that her platform allowed her to inter act with wanna-bes because he didn't trust anyone who lived outside the Lower End. "Ginny I'm for you, not your platform," he said.

"Charlie, we want the same things, too. Out of the Lower End," she said.

"Yea, but not at the cost of stepping on each other to get there. It doesn't have to be that way, Ginny."

"I know Charlie, and I promise it won't be that way for me."

"Good. You and Addie can do it, just don't forget who you are. You're different Ginny, you can make it out, without selling out," he said. His words inspired her to keep her dream alive, to someday leave the Lower End. She and Addie, Charlie's older sister and her best friend, always talked about how they were going to get out- unmarried, pregnant free, and not as a wanna-be. She and Addie were going to use their minds and convictions at a college.

Charlie encouraged their ambition and often cautioned Ginny to stay clear of wanna-be guys. He said, "Ginny don't trust anybody who thinks they're better than you." She laughed, and told Charlie, "I can take care of myself. I'm not as gullible as you think. I don't need protecting, Charlie Meaks."

The sound grew faint, and Ginny was finding out how much she needed Charlie's protection, as a shadow crept across the wall. "Reveal your self," she whispered. Out of the shadow, he appeared. Pausing, he looked around the dimly lit room. Up against the wall, he saw her frightened face. He didn't move towards her, instead he reached out his hand to her. Ginny's frightened body gave way to the safety of his touch. His rapid heartbeat vibrated through her entire body as he rocked her side to side, "Shhh, I've gotten rid of him. You need to hurry, get the baby and your things together. Only bring what you and the baby need," he said. Releasing her tight grip, Ginny did as he said. He pulled her back into his arms and her body leaned into his. She lifted her face up to him. He used his palms to pat away tears on her cocoa skin. Charlie tenderly smiled at her as he gently let her go to pack their things. He walked to the living room window of his second story one-bedroom apartment overlooking a busy intersection. Aimlessly, he stared at the streets of Denver, Colorado. Without awareness to his own voice, "Dear God, where will we go?" His question echoed out into the dawning sky as he picked up the phone.

"Hello."

"Addie, there isn't much time to explain. I'm taking Ginny and the baby away in . . .," Addie tried to interrupt, but her voice was overpowered by Charlie's non-stop talk about his intents. "Please Sis . . . "

"What's going on? I've been waiting to hear from you, Charlie."

"Now isn't the time for questions," Charlie said rubbing his forehead. "If I don't take Ginny and the baby away, he'll take her . . . you know he will." Addie attempted to interrupt, but was overpowered again. "Please Sis, just listen. I know what's best."

"Haven't you heard Charlie?" she yelled over his husky voice, "About two hours ago, it was on the news. Oh, dear Lord . . . he's dead! He's dead! Don't you know? He's dead Charlie!"

"What are you talking about? Who's dead?" he shouted into the receiver.

"Rowan. He's dead Charlie. Ro . . . Rowan . . . he's dead. Somebody killed him," she hysterically responded. Stillness filled the dawning cold air as Charlie silently listened to his sister. "Charlie . . . he's dead. The police found his body an hour or so ago. It's all over the news. Didn't you know Charlie?"

Charlie took a deep breath as he closed his eyes. His left hand went limp and the other held the phone like a crutch. His body swayed and he attempted to speak. His mouth moved without sound, as he wiped away moisture from his forehead. Dumbfounded, he shook his head side to side. His sister's revelation clouded his thinking. He knew Rowan was alive when he dumped his unconscious body in an alley on the other side of town. The past four hours replayed through his mind. Charlie retraced every step of the argument and fight, right up to the moment he hit Rowan over the head to dumping his unconscious body. Ginny walked into the room. She immediately knew something was wrong by the way, his thumb and index finger rested on his forehead. "What is it?" she asked, "Who are you talking to?" He didn't respond. The raging sounds and images of his struggle with Rowan caused him to ramble about what happened. Everything he thought and felt was clouded by his sister's announcement. His high school rival one of Denver's black community favorite sons, a wanna-be was dead. Startled by her grabbing at the phone he shoved Ginny away.

"Addie . . . you've got to . . . we've got to get a handle on this thing. We gotta . . . we gotta pull ourselves together. There aren't any choices left. Ginny," he said as he looked into her frightened eyes, "the baby and I are leaving Denver right now! I don't know what's going on . . . I just don't know." His burdened voice raised the inescapable question, "If I wait around they might think I . . ."

"Think what Charlie? You said you were only going to talk to him. What happened Charlie? What will they think?" she softly questioned her beloved younger brother. "Charlie, what will they think?" she asked again holding one hand over her heart.

"Nothing else matters anymore. Remember everything we talked about, only one thing has to change. Don't try to find us Addie . . . don't ever try to find us." The next sound she heard was the dial tone echoing through the phone. Addie's shaking hand was unable to replace the phone in its cradle, so she used her other hand to steady herself as she gently placed it down in its cradle. She slumped down into an old reclining chair, leaning back into the thickness of its back, her nails dug into the old torn itchy fabric. The vibration of the fabric crunched as she dragged her fingers across it, breaking the silence in the room. Addie closed her eyes and prayed for them, "Dear Lord, keep'em. Especially, the baby, Heavenly Father. Protect her 'cause she's the only innocent one."

Charlie turned to face Ginny. He reached out to pull her close to him, but she hesitated. "Don't Ginny," he said as tears swelled in his eyes. "I love you and the baby. I swear to you everything is all right," he said reaching for her again. Never diverting away from his gaze, slowly she took his hand and lead him to the front door where their bags were waiting.

"Good morning, US Army Recruiting office, Sergeant First Class Mills speaking. How may I help you?"

"Hello Mark, it's me."

"What a nice surprise. How are you?"

"I'm doing fine. I wanted to speak to you about someone. Her name is Areesa. She's a student of mine. Her parents died three weeks ago in a car accident. She's a young lady who needs a change, so I'd like to suggest to her that she gets in touch with you."

"Sorry to hear about her loss. She must really need a change if you're calling me."

"Yes she does. I remember how alone I was before signing on for active duty. She's bright, strong, and what's the word you use all the time?"

"Motivated."

"Yea motivated," she replied with a smirk on her face.

"What's her background, besides being a college student? Do you think she's up for it?"

"I believe she is." She paused and thought to herself, "I just have to convince her she is."

"OK, why don't you send her to my office and I'll see what I can do. Tell her what it's all about. Don't hold anything back."

"Sounds good. Thanks Mark."

"How's life treating you?"

"Fine. And yourself?"

"I'm ok."

"Well, take care Mark. Bye-bye."

"Out," he said.

A FEW DAYS LATER . . .

This was the second of many interventions in Areesa's life, a sophomore college student majoring in communication. She was an only child and a loner who enjoyed talking about the world. Although she lived in many places, most of what she knew was from books. Her favorite college professor was Ms. Mills, who often said to her, "How is it that you are so well traveled, but you don't realize that you are?" Areesa just smiled about her unusual observation, and told her she would have to ask her parents. After her parents' deaths, she had no one except Ms. Mills who turned out to also be a good friend.

"Areesa, please wait after class. I'd like to speak with you."

"Sure Ms. Mills." Areesa was very special to her and she did everything she could to support her throughout this terrible time in her life.

"Hey Lady, I was surprised to see you in class. I'm especially impressed with all the work you've turned in today. You don't have to rush you know. It's only been three weeks and a couple of days since your parents' deaths."

"I'm really trying to stay busy," she said not wanting to blink her eyes because she knew her tears would fall. "Sometimes I find myself walking in a building, down a street, or in our house and I'm thinking of them, as if they aren't dead. I miss them. You know we shared everything," she said, pointing to herself, "had I not gotten the opportunity to say good-bye to them before their deaths . . .," she paused and took a deep breath, "Staying busy is the best thing for me right now." Not wanting to cry, but unable to control her falling tears, she covered her face with her hands to muffle her sobbing.

"It's OK to cry whenever you feel you have to. Just cry honey. Cry until your eyes run dry. And remember your parents and every moment you shared together. You know, I found out a long time ago, the only way to deal with grief is to get it out. Out into the open. Most people ignore it. They turn to other things, like drugs, pills, alcohol, the wrong crowd. Even worse, they act like nothing is wrong to avoid facing their problems. But when you know things are not the way they should be, it takes more courage to face the problem than it does to ignore it. You're strong and I know someday your pain is going to become easier to bear." She waited a moment before bringing up her suggestion about enlisting into the Army because sometimes Areesa seemed so easily broken. Though Ms. Mill's heart felt comfortably nitched in her throat, she raised her question.

"I have a recommendation, but I want you to hear me out before you respond."

"All right, what is it?"

"Oh, don't look so frightened," she said looking into her teary eyes. "Have you ever considered the Armed Forces as an occupation?" she quickly ranted off.

"The what?"

"The Armed Forces. You know. Uniforms, guns - bang*bang - Private Benjamin, the military. The Army," she responded to Areesa's baffled look.

"No! I've never thought about going into the Army or anything like it. Why would I?"

"Hold on and hear me out before you write me off as crazy. The Army has a lot of advantages. To name a few - security, decent money and excellent benefits. You'll get a chance to grow and learn about who you are. It'll change you in ways you've never thought of and you'll learn to face new challenges with a sense of self." She paused from her sales pitch. She knew convincing her was a one-time shot. "Now, I know your parents didn't leave much money for you," she stated hesitantly as she continued to monitor Areesa's reactions. "Yes, you have the house, but how will you maintain the house and keep up your studies? The Army will take care of these things. Uncle Sam, Uncle Daddy, or Uncle Sugar, whichever you prefer, will give you a check twice a month and throw in some educational opportunities. Educational programs unmatched by other organizations. I'm sure you're asking, how do I know so much about this? Well, prior to teaching, I served for ten years. While on active duty, I met my ex-husband Mark, who is now a recruiter. If it wasn't for the educational programs, I wouldn't be here on this campus teaching you Social Anthropology." She waited for some feedback, but Areesa's moistened face remained blank and unresponsive. Ms. Mills pressed forward with her campaign to get Areesa enlisted. "Give it a try. I strongly believe it'll be a good thing for you. I can go on and on about why you should look into this. One major factor to consider Areesa is you need to feel like you belong. And getting a degree is not what you need right now. What you need is to feel a sense of companionship and I believe you can fulfill this need to belong by going into the Army. After a year or so, you'll feel better equipped to handle your studies, work, and a house. Honey, I can't think," she said placing her index finger on her temple, "of a better place to find good friends and yourself."

The quietness in the classroom was awkward. The two sat quietly, patiently pondering. Ms. Mills didn't know what Areesa was thinking, though she was wondering about what would be said next. Seated behind her desk, she looked into Areesa's face for a clue, about how she was going to respond and she was also thinking about how she was going to counter her objections, but Areesa's face remained indifferent, like she was a thousand miles away. For the first time since knowing Areesa, Ms. Mills wondered if Areesa had heard anything, she said. "Areesa are you still here with me?" She nodded yes. Ms. Mills opened her desk drawer and retrieved a lime green stick-um pad and a pen, then she scribbled Mark's name and telephone number on it. She walked from behind her desk towards Areesa, and opened her hand, placing the small piece of paper in it, then wrapped both their hands around the paper. "Areesa, I don't want to pretend I know exactly what you're feeling. I can only offer my support to you. You know you can always count on me for the truth. In saying that, I know you need to discover a new world and yourself, *without your parents.*" Areesa looked up at her, and as always, Ms. Mills was awed by her beautiful dark bottomless eyes. In that moment, Ms. Mills knew she would never forget how lost Areesa looked sitting on top of that desk looking up at her with visible tear trails on her chestnut skin as her mink mane rested below her shoulders. "Please Honey, for yourself, take this opportunity and see where it leads you," she said trying to control her trembling voice as she held Areesa's hands in her own. Areesa cleared her throat as she attempted to speak, but no words came. Ms. Mills believed Areesa understood her intentions were good, but unknowingly, Ms. Mills unctioning was creating more uncertainty for her. Areesa felt sad because she knew she couldn't explain how she felt she was a victim of something beyond her control. As her teacher continued to speak, Areesa recalled her last moments with her Mom.

"Mommy, rest. We'll talk in the morning." Ginny's determination to speak wouldn't let her rest, or close her eyes.

"Areesa, always remember it was our love for you that drove us to lead our lives the way we did. We wanted you to have friends and so much more, it's just," Ginny turned her head and held her stomach because she didn't want Areesa to see how painful it was to cough. "We wanted, so much for you . . . so much. There's something you must know . . . your father and I kept this from you for too long. I wish we were having this talk for other reasons. Now I'm dying and I . . . oh, my precious baby, I love you so much. I need you to forgive us, forgive me Baby for the choices we made."

"Mommy no. Please just rest. When you wake up tomorrow, everything will be ok. Everything is going to be OK," she said crying into her mother's warm, comforting hand, "I can't do this, I can't. Mommy please don't leave me too," she cried lifting her head up towards heaven.

"Now-now Baby, you're going to be fine. I already know. God has kept us all this time, in spite of . . ., Baby, He's not going to turn His back. But, He wants me to finally let honor into your life. You've grown up in the gloom of lies. Lingering lies," she said half smiling, "you were always ok with it and you didn't even know what it was. So remember you're a strong person Areesa. Always remember your Daddy and I love you." Areesa cried as Ginny struggled to speak. "We made choices. Hard, difficult choices during that time in our lives, but don't you fear the past, like we did 'cause it'll shadow the rest of your life. Areesa, are you listening?"

"Mommy, I'm trying to," she said moving her head up and down, trying to stop crying so she could hear her Mom's voice. She didn't want to ever not hear her Mom's voice.

"Look through my things for the name Addie and call her. She'll have all the answers you'll need to sort this out. Areesa, promise me you'll call her." Ginny waited. Areesa, reluctantly said yes. Ginny smiled at her obedience. How she loved her only child, her baby. Her rising star. Ginny died during the night as Areesa sat next to her bed holding her warm hand.

Now, weeks later, sitting in a classroom with her favorite teacher the sound of her mother's voice asking her to keep a promise haunted her.

"Areesa. Areesa, are you ok?" Ms. Mills asked. Without a word Areesa simply stood up, walked passed Ms. Mills, and out of the classroom.

... she decided

The training area was surrounded by a lush canopy of evergreen pine and deciduous oak trees. The entrance read: Welcome to Fort McCellan Basic and Advance Training Post. After arriving at the reception station new soldiers were picked up by a representative of their platoon. Areesa disembarked the olive green school bus at a three-story brownstone with three front entrances and exit doors on the left and right ends of the building. The entire campus consisted of similar three story buildings that reminded her of better kept Projects.

Areesa entered the front door on the far left end of the building. As she entered, the smell of pine-oil and wax penetrated her nostrils. She looked down at her image reflected in the waxed floor. Amazed, she shook her head in disbelief of the floor's mirror ability. The hall's walls and staircase were free of dust, and spotlessly in appearance. She was in awe of the sterile surroundings, as she slowly walked further into the building looking up, down, and around, as her footsteps echoed throughout the stairwell. Shyly she peeped around the rail at the four remaining flights of stairs above her. Her footsteps' echo continuously bounced off the eggshell colored walls despite her attempts to walk without making any sound up to the third floor.

Two gray doors stood between her and her sleeping quarters. She pulled the heavy gray doors open with both hands, as her backpack fell from her shoulder onto the floor creating another echoing sound that resonated down the stairwell. She picked it up and stepped onto the floor. Amazed by the cold imposing still hall, that seemed to stretch forever; she stayed still while taking it all in. She cleared her throat, and the faint sound reverberated then disappeared. To her left were two swinging doors with Alpha 1-5 written above them and on the restaurant like doors one said "In" the other "Out". A lounging area was in the middle of the long hall along with what appeared to be two offices to the left of the lounging area, and two pay phones on the right side wall. One phone receiver had Alpha written on it, the other read Bravo. Next to the phones was a door, with Cadre Latrine Only written cross it in bold black letters. Above the two restaurant doors on the opposite end of the hall, a sign hung above it that read: Bravo 1-5. "I'm Alpha," said as she turned to her left and entered the swinging doors.

Areesa shivered after stepping into the huge opposing room. There were fifteen beds on the left side and fifteen on the right. This room was known as a Bay. Next to each bed, there was a six-foot high locker. The lockers had brown metal panels on each of the front doors. A towel rack was inside every locker along with a fiber class mirror and five wire hangers. Each locker had a small dresser with three drawers inside it. A key-lock with the word "Temp" hung on the outside of the locker. At the foot of each bed was an olive-drab wooden footlocker containing two trays that lay on top of an open compartment and a key-lock laid in the bottom with "Temp" also written on it. The gray steel beds were made-up with two wool olive-drab blankets. One blanket lay across the pillow double folded and the other covered the bunk with tightly tucked ninety-degree hospital corners. "Wow," Areesa said, "I guess Ms. Mills forgot to tell me about the great luxuries."

Areesa dropped her backpack at the first bed and took a tour of the area. The scent of pine oil and wax became stronger as she approached the rear of the cold huge room. The first door had the word latrine written across the top in black letters. She gently pushed the door open and stuck her head in to inspect. She pushed the door open further after she recognized the familiar place - it was a bathroom. The bathroom's sterile image emanated the strongest smell of pine oil. A row of twelve white sinks and matching mirrors lined the right side of the wall. On the left side there were twelve toilets enclosed by gray stalls. The bathroom floor tile, made of miniature squares with specks of light blue, dark blue, and powder blue matched the blue walls. On the far end of the right wall, Areesa was shocked by an open room. She became discouraged about her desire to stay and her decision to enlist, even more. "No, they didn't! No this can't be real. I'm going to kill you Ms. Mills," Areesa voice echoed through the "open" shower.

The open shower walls were brown with light brown tiles. Hanging from the center of the ceiling was what looked like a large showerhead with branches that branched off into five extended shower nozzles. No curtains. No dividers. Just walls and pipes. Positioned on the right and left sides of the wall, hot and cold-water controls stuck out. As she walked out of the stall, laughing at her dilemma, the loss of all privacy, she swung her arms up into the air letting them drop freely. She accidentally hit the button on her right side. One of the extended nozzles squirted out a burst of water that caught the back of her hair and clothes. The coldwater spray chilled her back causing her to jump and scream. "I'm going to kill you Ms. Mills!" Her voice echoed back, I'm going to kill . . ., "Oh shut up," she shouted back at her echo.

She walked over to the sink, grabbed several brown stiff paper towels, and tried to dry her clothes and hair.

Without thought to time, she journeyed into the room next to the latrine. Inside this room, washers were lined up side-by-side on the left and dryers on the right. In the rear of the room, there were two large deep sinks mounted on the wall below silver shelves that shone brightly, reflecting anything that neared them. Behind the door, on hooks were mops that reeked the smell of pine oil. Behind the door was a buffer that smelled like the other strong distinctive smell throughout the entire building, acrylic wax. She tossed the damp brown paper towels into a gray trash can that came up to her waist. She was amazed that everything was big, shiny and organized. She leaned backwards on the door and fell out of the laundry room, and stumbled in to a door with a red and white neon exit sign above it.

The balcony was enclosed by a brick wall that came as high as her chest. Red cans with the word "BUTTS" rested in each corner of the balcony and the stairs were encased by high rails leading down to a courtyard. She hoisted herself up hip even with the wall, to watch the soldiers below doing marching exercises. She awkwardly lowered herself down and landed on a red "BUTTS" can. She made a disgusting face about a habit she was taught to dislike. She leaned against the wall, and stared aimlessly at the tree line surrounding the training area. Before she realized it weepiness filled her heart, and she was crying, overwhelmed by memories of her parents' sudden death. "Mommy, who is Addie? I don't know if I can keep this promise. I'm afraid Mommy," she cried. She reached into her pocket and pulled out a piece of paper that read: Addie Meaks, Denver, Colorado, 303-555-0204. She crumpled the paper and attempted to throw it over the wall, but couldn't. She knew she wouldn't break the last promise she made to her mother. Accepting her promise, she pushed the crumpled paper back into her pocket. She got up, brushed her denims off and re-entered the balcony door into the Bay.

Unaware of her pace or the presence of anyone else in the Bay, Areesa bumped into a man wearing an Army camouflaged uniform and a Smoky the Bear brown hat with a gold emblem in the center. Startled, she jumped back, clearly shaken from bumping into him. The Drill Sergeant didn't move out of his position. He was poised, broad, and solid at five feet, eleven inches. She thought, "No wonder he didn't budge." The Drill Sergeant stood firm as she looked up at him. Her eyes traced over his clean-shaven sable complexion, etched check bones, neatly trimmed mustache that faded off at the sides of his full lips. His dark piercing eyes were proportioned in size to fit his handsome face. His high and tight fade hair cut revealed shaven hairs just below the rim of his large round hat. He didn't speak, he only stared down at her slender frame. She responded to the hold of his stare with a subtle smile. Intimidated, she stuttered as she attempted to apologize for not paying attention to where she was going. "Hi, I . . . I was just out on the - the balcony, looking, and . . .," she said pointing towards the balcony door.

"Out on the balcony looking?" he rudely interrupted.

"Yes, looking," she repeated.

"Soldier didn't you hear the call for a formation to go to chow?" he shouted. Areesa was shocked by his demeanor. Her oval eyes grew large, and she tried to maintain her composure as he verbally exploded, as she thought "You're the one who nearly knocked me on the floor, what are you so mad about?"

"Soldier you've got about ten seconds to get out of my sight and down to the Dining Hall. And the next time I catch you *out on the balcony*," he said mocking her mannerism, "on my time, I'll have you doin' push- ups until this training sight begins to shake! Do you understand me Private?" he bellowed at her.

"I just, I . . ."

"You just what? What don't you un-der-stand, Private?" Areesa pulled her face back from the rim of his hat that came within an inch of touching her head. She rushed pass him confused, hurt, and frightened. She pushed through the doors and hurried down the stairs onto the platform leading outside. The Drill Sergeant yelled at her from an unseen window, "Double time, Soldier! You better pick your feet up and start moving in a running motion. Now, double time." For a few seconds she couldn't hear him anymore, then suddenly she heard, "I'm watching you. I wanna see you running until you get to the Dinning Hall," he yelled. Areesa began running as fast as her legs would go until she stumbled. Like a gymnast, she struggled to stay on her feet by hopping and then landing into a crouched position. She stood up, and then looked around to see if anyone had seen her. "That's enough!" she yelled aloud, not caring who heard her.

Areesa arrived at the Dining Hall. She took her place at the end of the chow line. Everyone stood still, one behind the other, facing forward with their eyes directed at the back of the person's head in front of them. Some were in uniforms and some, like her, were still wearing civilian clothes. They all stood with their heels shoulder length apart and their palms facing outward, resting in the small of their backs. She wondered if anyone could see she had been crying. She felt a need to blow her nose. She didn't want to draw attention to herself, so she faked clearing her throat as she quickly rubbed her nose, praying no fragments of dried flakes would appear on the back of her hand. She went too fast, so she did it again. She dropped her hand quickly and breathed a breath of relief, no white flakes and no Drill Sergeant up in her face asking what she was doing. She leaned over and looked up the line, watching the Drill Sergeant who busted-her-out, take a seat behind the table with a stack of cafeteria trays on it. She peeped out again to see how much space was between him and the trays. It wasn't much. "I'm going to kill . . . you . . . Ms. Mills," she grumbled. As she moved closer to the front of the line, she was shocked, but not surprised, by another life changing rule the Army imposed upon her and all the other poor souls crazy enough to take someone's advice and enlist.

"One Drill Ser-geant!"

"Two Drill Ser-geant!"

"Three Drill Ser-geant!"

"Four Drill Ser-geant!"

"Five Drill Ser-geant!"

Each trainee sounded-off as he or she approached the sign-in table before getting a cafeteria tray. The repetitious calling began again, from one to five. All soldiers in training, known as trainees, did this to assist the Drill Sergeants with a head count to determine how many soldiers were eating in the Dining Hall. "Really. Ms. Mills, I'm through with you!" Areesa thought to her self when once again she was caught off guard because she wasn't listening to what number was previously called, leaving her clueless as to what her number was. She found herself standing toe-to-toe, face to chest with Drill Sergeant A. Patterson, again. "Pity is my only hope," she thought to herself when she decided to cry and run, embarrassed, out of the Dining Hall if he treated her the way he did earlier. Felling overwhelmed, over stimulated she dropped her head and waited for an explosion to escape this man as she stood before him so frightened she was afraid to look at him.

"What's your number Private?" he calmly asked.

"I don't know, Drill Sergeant," she whispered.

"Two," he responded. She looked up at him. He was close enough for her to smell his starched uniform and cologne. She subtly bit her bottom lip while making a soft sigh. She lowered her head, staring at the floor, trying, to avoid eye contact with him.

"Two, Drill Sergeant," she whispered. Drill Sergeant A. Patterson didn't move immediately, but he maintained his position looking down at her loose black hair draping forward, covering her face. She tilted her head back to look into his face, and then he stepped to one side and let her pass. She hesitated, then moved ahead to get a tray and proceed through the line.

"You can have anything you want, including the cook," a tall slender guy advised her.

"No thanks," she said smiling, "I'll just have the burger." She looked over her shoulder, anticipating another glimpse of the Drill Sergeant, but he was gone.

. . . meet your buddy

"Male on the floor," Drill Sergeant West bawled out. Female bodies scattered towards beds and underneath itchy wool-olive-drab blankets. Some hid barely clothed bodies in the latrine or laundry room, while others used their six-foot locker doors to shielded their bodies. All revealed their heads to hear his indifferent tenor voice.

"Listen up. Formation is tomorrow at 0-6-30 hours. You will not be late for my formation! The uniform for the day is Battle Dress Uniform (camouflaged uniform). I won't repeat this long drawn out name again Josephines (a military nickname for female recruits), because it takes too much of my time. From this moment forward when I say BDUs, you will know I am referring to your newly issued, fashionable ensemble with coordinating head and foot wear."

"What if we don't have our BDUs?" someone asked.

"That's not difficult to figure out Josephine. Wear appropriate civilian attire until they are issued," he sarcastically stated. "You will fall-out in front of the double doors to your left and my right, outside of this building on the graveled area designated for Alpha 1-5, that's Alpha 1st Battalion, 5th Platoon formation area for the remainder of your stay," he said as he looked around, noticing all of their hiding places. He shook his head side to side and continued, "Tomorrow is going to be a busy one. Orientations, uniform issue, classes, and shots."

"Shots?" someone questioned.

"Yes, Josephines, shots. So get a good breakfast because you're going to need it. By the way. And don't fall out for my formations late, or you'll be giving me twenty-five male push-ups until *I* get tired."

This was Areesa, and the others', first *interactive* two-way conversation with Alpha 1-5 lead Drill Sergeant Robert West. Liking it or not, as he put it, he was now their father, mother, brother, sister, Nanny, and best friend. As he turned to leave, he stopped in his tracks and announced, "After I give you a block of instructions you-will-acknowledge your comprehension by sounding off with - ROCKY STEADY AL-PHA. Do you hear me?" The 30 member female platoon of all hues, sizes, and abilities yelled, "ROCKY STEADY AL-PHA."

"And another thing, if myself or Drill Sergeant Patterson, enter this Bay, the first Josephine, to see us had better yell male-on-the-floor, then at-ease, so all of you will know that either myself or another Drill is entering this Bay. I don't wanna see this again," he said pointing at their hiding places, "yall hiding in lockers and getting back into bunks. You all should sleep in appropriate clothing because if for some reason, any reason, Drill Sergeant Patterson or myself, have to come in here at night, the last thing either of us want to see are your tails hanging out. Let this be your last time by recognizing I mean what I say, and I say what I mean. Because believe me, you won't do it again, after being smoked. And if you don't know what it means to get smoked, mess with me and you will. Don't get caught after this day. You've been warned. As-you-were," he said spinning on his heels, leaving them mumbling about more rules. A female sergeant entered the bay and told them lights would be out in twenty minutes.

Areesa rested on her bed looking up at the ceiling, noticing for the first time that the ceiling was a dark gloomy gray, but the walls were eggshell. Go figure. Like when she arrived, it was raining and the Drill Sergeant told her to put her umbrella away because it rains on the Army, not in it. She lifted her knees up and crunched them to her chest, then sprang her legs out, and jumped up from her bunk. She bent her torso to her knees and let her arms hang and touch the floor, "I can do this. It's going to be ok. Mommy, it is going to be ok. Right?" she asked, as if waiting for a response. Only a cool breeze from an open door answered her as it whisked past her barely covered body. She stretched her arms out level with her shoulders. "Yep. No reply," she said grabbing her towel from her wall locker, then she headed for the latrine.

Areesa moved closer to the mirror, looking over her face. She moved her lips left, then right. She opened her mouth as wide as she could, inspecting her teeth and gums. Then, she pulled her hair up with one hand and inspected her neck and ears. Areesa realized she was transforming into a familiar image that she liked, her mom. With both hands on the sink, she leaned into the mirror. Her forehead thumped against the image containing the silhouette of her Mom. She recalled how her mom went through the same routine every morning, advising her to know her body inside and out. Areesa turned on the faucet, caught water in her cupped hands, then let it splash back into the sink, then used her wet palms to lightly pat water on her face attempting to hide her tears. She cupped her hands together again, caught more cold water and doused it over her face wetting her T-shirt and hairline. "Come on Areesa. Come on get it together. They're gone. They-are-gone."

The latrine door swung open and a young woman about Areesa's age strolled in. Areesa caught a glimpse of her through the mirror, but she didn't acknowledge her presence. She hoped the female had not heard her, and that she would quickly leave. The young woman walked in and out of stalls. "What happened to being a sweetie, and wiping the seat," she said. Areesa ignored her. She stood in front of the next stall, sticking her head inside. Annoyed by the musical stall game, Areesa closed her eyes and tried to block the female out.

The whooshing sound of the toilet made Areesa jump. Her body froze for a few seconds then relaxed as she looked around the latrine for the female. After realizing where the female was, Areesa set in her mind to ignore her. She was getting good at ignoring people and blocking everything out and retreating into her own world. Clogging her thoughts with emptiness was her way of dealing with her parents' deaths. The stall door opened and the young woman came out buckling her BDU pants. She walked over to the sink next to Areesa and began washing her hands.

"Of all the sinks in here she has to use this one. Goodness," Areesa thought to herself.

"Hi, I'm Private Tiffoni Stryker . . . nice to meet you and be here with you," she said extending her moist had for a handshake. Areesa looked at Tiffoni, then her wet outstretched hand. "I'm only kidding. You know, no one around here gets privacy. Since you were looking quite peaceful in your private world, I thought I would remind you of that," she said with a fake straight face. Areesa laughed. "Now that I know you haven't lost your mind, I'm Areesa Davis and I think it's nice to meet you too."

"I've been here for eight weeks. Yea. Really. Hey, don't look concerned. I got them right where I want them. No really, I do." Tiffoni said, assuredly. "I was in another company but I'm what they call a recycle. Can you believe it? Me. Recycled like an outdated newspaper. I couldn't pass the physical training so, here I am. Getting the royal opportunity to stay among the idiots under the big brown hats just a bit longer. But I like it, 'cause I got time."

"OK, you like it. At least one of us do," Areesa mumbled with toothpaste in her mouth. Tiffoni turned her back to the sink and lifted herself onto it, using it has a seat.

"My Dad is in."

"Really. So the whole family is nuts," she said washing her face with a warm cloth.

"We sure are. Right down to the maid." Areesa looked at Tiffoni from the corner of her eye without acknowledging her last remark. She realized, figuring out whether Tiffoni was playing or serious was going to keep her on her toes.

Tiffoni, a slender brownish-red out spoken twenty-two year old, was the direct opposite to Areesa's withdrawn behavior. Unlike Areesa, Tiffoni had no problem imposing her presence on anyone. Areesa thought she looked and acted as if she belonged at the one party everybody, who thought they were somebody, wanted to be at. She was curvy with shoulder length brown locks, large slanted eyes that squinted together when she talked. She had pretty, white straight teeth and full lips. A red-bone whose smile and stunning eyes, Areesa thought, made her look sneaky. In spite of her sassy attitude, which Areesa was not accustomed to, she liked her.

"Male on the floor," a female's voice yelled out.

"OK, ladies, formation in five minutes," a man's voice bellowed.

"Five minutes! I'm not dressed. I can't be late to another formation," Areesa yelled.

"I'll help. Where's your uniform?"

"On my bunk," she said pulling her hair up into a ponytail.

"I'll get it. What about your boots?"

"Oh yea. Under my bunk," Areesa managed to say with four bobby-pins sticking out of her mouth. She grabbed her comb and toothbrush and rushed out of the latrine. She met Tiffoni in the center of the bay grabbing her BDU pants as Tiffoni attempted to put on her shirt at the same time. Areesa reached for one of her boots, to put it on as she turned to put her other arm in her BDU shirt. Then she slipped her other foot into a lone boot in the center of the floor. Tiffoni tied one boot while Areesa tied the other. They both leaped to their feet and began running for the double doors leading out to the hallway. Tiffoni let the weight of her body fall onto the next door, leading to the stairs. Areesa ran through the open door, leaping into the air, landing on the second step with Tiffoni on her heels. They took the remaining stairs two at a time. Their boots echoed as they landed in a gymnast position on the first floor landing. Both of them slammed against the double doors leading outside as Drill Sergeant A. Patterson, called the platoon to attention. Areesa and Tiffoni took deep breaths and fell-in at the back of the formation.

"Privates Stryker and Davis why are you late for my formation?"

"No reason Drill Sergeant," Tiffoni yelled back.

"Right," he said shaking his head up and down, "No reason. Well, seeing that Private Davis is making a habit of this, I think I'd better do something about it. What do you think about that Private Stryker?"

"I don't know Drill Sergeant," Tiffoni said looking into Areesa's watery eyes. She moved her shoulders up and down, not knowing where the conversation was going.

"That's what they pay me for Private. Because it is my job to know. Stryker, do you believe it is my job to ensure, you know what I know?" Overriding her voice he said, "What I know is this. From this day forward, you two are Buddies. Where I see one - I'd better see the other."

"Yes, Drill Ser-geant," the two of them yelled out.

"Good. Now DROP and give me fifteen push-ups. That goes for the two of you. If one drops, so will the other. And prior to getting on your feet, you will request permission to recover," he said approaching them. "You will say: Thank you Drill Sergeant for conditioning my mind and my body. Please feel free to do so at anytime. Say-your-name, Private Davis, request permission to recover," he turned and walked back to the front of the platoon. Still down in the push-up position, Tiffoni stretched her head back as far as she could letting her back sink close to the ground to relieve the pressure in her trembling arms.

"Areesa,"

"Yea,"

"The sky is pretty isn't it?" Areesa looked at her from her uncomfortable position wondering what it was going to mean, being linked with her for eight weeks.

"I guess."

"Hey. Welcome to the United States Army."

Areesa, Tiffoni, and the others' day muddled along, and they were all, vulnerable to long-winded Drill Sergeants, drawn-out classes about not doing this, can't do that, and rules and more rules. Whenever Areesa was beginning to feel the Drill Sergeants couldn't get any worse, they'd do something to top themselves.

After breakfast, the platoon arrived at the Troop Medical Center (TMC) for shots. They were ordered to line up in a single file. All of them could see into the large open sterile and spotlessly hygienic room. Four medics, two on the left, the other two on the right stood waiting for them just pass the door threshold. They were operating hand held robotic shot administering guns, with needles sticking out of them, which appeared to be as long as their arms! She pondered, how can a person be brave, when they have to willingly walk through those doors with both of their sleeves up, to take two shots at one time and not want to faint. "Unreal. Simply unreal," Areesa said as she prayed for her body, mind, and spirit to not, leave her during a time when her spirit was willing but her flesh was not.

As she witnessed private, after private, after private break into crying fits overwhelmed by fear fall-out of the line, prepared to accept whatever consequences the Drills dished out, she knew this was not an option for her and Tiffoni. DROP. Drop. Drop. When they heard the word, they knew to hit the floor and start knocking out push-ups. Drill Sergeant A. Patterson consistently dropped them at the least little thing one of them did. Talking. Laughing. Smiling. He dropped them both. They were sitting quietly, minding their own business when he accused them of bringing the spirits of the entire platoon down. Wrong turns. Right turns. For running when they should've been walking and walking when they should've been running. DROP. Even if he thought they were thinking of doing something, he'd drop them. All day, even when they weren't together he'd drop one and make the other call out to inform the other she had to drop too.

In spite of his constant aggravating commands and demands, she found herself staring at him. She wondered what the "A" stood for in front of his last name. She even thought of first names for him. "Alvin. No. Too corny. Aaron. Nope, too starchy. Abraham, definitely not, too biblical . . ."

"Whatcha smiling at Davis?" Tiffoni asked.

"Nothing."

"Yea, right. Nothing."

The Platoon arrived back at the barracks at six o'clock in the evening. Areesa and all the others were exhausted. She and Tiffoni remained in the shower an extra ten minutes letting the soothing hot water run on their shoulders and backs. She couldn't recall her body ever being so sore. In the mean time, Drill Sergeant A. Patterson came into the Bay while they were still in the shower and moved Tiffoni's bed next to Areesa. He was really tripping on the Buddy thing, but they didn't mind this time because they were going to ask to switch them around anyway. "Later Buddy, I'm exhausted. See you at o-dark-thirty," Tiffoni said as she left the latrine. Areesa remained behind gathering her things, and memories of her parents stirred her tired mind. She wondered what her parents would think about her possibly selling the house, dropping out of college and enlisting in to the Army.

"Mommy, I miss you. Almost two months has gone by since you and Dad … it still feels like yesterday. I hope you guys approve of my decision. There's no one to ask anymore. No. There isn't," she thought as she lay across her bed and wrapped her arms around herself. She slid under the covers and pulled her blanket up over her face. She didn't want anyone to hear her crying. She squeezed her eyes shut, but the tears continued to come.

Areesa quietly slipped on her robe and slippers that were beneath her bed. As she stood, she looked down at Tiffoni who was sleeping peacefully. She walked through the Bay on the tip of her toes to the balcony exit door. Very quietly, she pushed the door open and stepped into the night air. She looked at the stars, a brilliant backdrop for the majestic tree line that went as far as her eyes could see. A cool evening breeze brushing against her wet face calmed her crying.

"Mommy, I'm so scared. I don't know if I belong here. I don't know where I'm going. The world is lonely without you and Dad." Areesa slid down the wall landing on her bottom. She wrapped her arms around her knees and cried freely, unconcerned about who might hear her. She didn't hear anyone coming up the stairs. "Are you OK?" a man's voice questioned. Startled by his presence she tensed up, pressing her back against the wall. She sat still fixing her eyes on his shadowy outline. She squinted her eyes trying to figure out who he was, but her teary eyes and the darkness kept her vision from identifying the man's face.

"Yes. I'm OK. Just a little home sick," she said sniffling, trying to see the man's face who sat down two stairs below her.

"It'll get easier," he paused. "Give yourself time. You'll see. After a little while it won't seem like a big deal." That voice, she knew that voice. He was dressed differently - in civilian clothing, but it was him, Drill Sergeant A. Patterson. Areesa sprung to her feet pulling her robe tightly around herself. Startled by her actions, he stood to his feet too.

"Drill Sergeant Patterson, I - I, couldn't sleep . . . I know I'm not supposed to be out here. I - I . . . I just couldn't sleep. I promise I won't be out here again," she said in one breath. She quickly turned, grabbed the door handle, swung the door open, and rushed back inside where the rest of her platoon were sound asleep.

shattered legacy

"Get up lazy, rise and shine," Tiffoni said frantically shaking Areesa, "Sergeant Patterson wants a formation right now. Get up or you're going to be late again."

"Sergeant Patterson called a formation. For real? No- I can't be late again. Not after last night," Areesa said, jumping out of bed rushing towards her locker, as Tiffoni quietly sat on her bunk snickering.

"There's no formation, it's Saturday," Tiffoni said as her giggling mixed with the laughter of the other girls in the platoon, who were sprawled across the Bay floor laughing hysterically. Areesa, embarrassed, stomped off to the latrine. Tiffoni ran after her. "Areesa. Bud-dy," she said trying to conceal her amusement. Areesa snatched away from her spilling toiletries into the sink. "Don't even go there, Tiffoni. Don't ever do that to me again, or you can be your own Buddy. Bud-dy."

"Hey slow down. I only wanted you to get up so we could go shopping at the PX (Post Exchange, the military's version of an on-post JC Penney). I didn't mean to get you upset," Tiffoni said with her hands held up in the stop position. Areesa wasn't amused by Tiffoni's antics. She also didn't like it when Tiffoni loud talked someone, or when she snickered at them behind their back after smiling in their face. It made her not trust Tiffoni. Most of the time it was innocent, but sometimes she did it to prove to everyone that she was the center of attention. Areesa was visibly agitated because she allowed Tiffoni's lack of good judgment to upset her like it did. She was normally accepting of situations like this. Before her parents' deaths she would have laughed along with the joke then ran home humiliated, telling them how cruel some kid had been to her. "I'm sorry," Tiffoni said with her head bowed. Without responding Areesa began washing her face. After brushing her teeth she still did not acknowledge Tiffoni, she walked passed her into a stall. She opened the gray door to come out and Tiffoni was standing in front of her.

"Move, Stryker."

"I said I'm sorry! what more do you want?"

"Nothin'."

"Buddies?"

"Maybe," Areesa said pushing pass her.

"What did you mean by, not after last night?"

"I was caught outside last night by Drill Sergeant Patterson."

"Going AWOL, ugh? I thought we agreed we'd subject ourselves to a few more name callings, push-ups, rules . . .," Tiffoni said jokingly as Areesa interrupted her role call.

"I'm serious. I couldn't believe it."

"OK, so what happened? Did he drop you? Wait let me guess. Apparently not, he didn't come and wake me up to get down with you. Or should I expect to do twenty-five push ups today?" Areesa laughed.

"You'd deserve it. I didn't give him a chance to say anything. I tried explaining, but I was so afraid of what he'd do, I just ran back inside."

"Seriously, between the two of us this Post has been pushed down at least two inches," Tiffoni said. "Hurry up. If we stay clear of him, maybe he'll forget all about last night." Tiffoni paused, and for the first time she attempted to find out what was with Areesa, all the sadness, making her cry, often forcing her to sit alone and stare with a blank expression on her face. "Areesa, by the way . . . why were you outside?"

"No reason," Areesa said, turning away quickly to avoid eye contact with Tiffoni.

"Next time you better think twice before going outside. Because you know Buddy, when you get down . . ."

"I get down," they said laughing.

HOURS LATER . . .

Areesa rode the entire way to the PX in silence, as Tiffoni chatted with everyone, especially the guys who were captivated by her looks and sassy attitude. Areesa lost herself in her thoughts. This time they were not filled with her parents' death, but with curiosity about his first name. She was sure whatever it was it fitted him. She liked the way his rage and calm attitude got things done. "So, the "A" has to stand for all of that. Sooo, it's Arnold. No, Allan. No, Armond, no that's too out there, but then so is he," she giggled. She didn't want Tiffoni to know she was thinking about him, so she held her head down to conceal her smile. He was nice to her out on the balcony. The last thing she ever expected from him. Areesa sighed. Then she drew in a deep breath, remembering how good he smelled. "Come on girl, snap out of it. One escape from the wrath of Drill Sergeant A. Patterson isn't grounds to get happy. Because you know, the only reason he didn't yell was because no one was there to hear him humiliate you," Areesa thought, sadly, to herself. She didn't notice the shuttle had stopped in front of the PX, until Tiffoni grabbed her by the arm, pulling her off the bus. After stepping off the bus, she realized

Tiffoni was laughing at her. Areesa stopped. She pulled away from Tiffoni's grip, and watched her and the rest of the group walk inside the PX.

The PX aviary entrance was a food court adorned with huge hanging ferns, large tropical trees, tables and chairs, and several fast food restaurants. The food court was surrounded by vendors, selling specialized merchandise to soldiers and their families. For them the PX was one stop shopping and the best thing going for trainees, because they were restricted to Post.

"Let's eat first. I want a Franks Frank. What do you want Areesa?"

"I want Hot Wok."

"You would." Areesa looked at Tiffoni, as to say what's wrong with Chinese food. But, she already knew what Tiffoni would say, that she was as conservative, or better yet, as corny as the food she liked.

"Tiffoni, order for me. I need to make a phone call."

"Who are you calling, Drill Sergeant Patterson?" she teased.

"Give it a rest, Tiffoni," Areesa replied as she walked across the colonnade to the pay phones. Once at the phone she looked for Tiffoni, who appeared sporadically from behind other soldiers and patrons. She wanted to keep a careful eye on her because she knew Tiffoni would order them both hot dogs wanting Areesa to experience what she was having. Areesa dropped the initial coin into the phone and waited for an operator. She saw Tiffoni sit down. Areesa jumped up and down trying to see if Tiffoni purchased what she wanted. Tiffoni saw her and held up the container with the Hot Wok logo on it. Areesa smiled.

"AT&T, how may I help you?"

"A person to person call," Areesa informed the operator.

"Your call will take an additional two dollars and fifty cents for the first three minutes." Areesa dropped the money into the slot.

"Who is the person you would like to speak with?"

"Addie Meaks," Areesa said licking her lips as she starred around trying not to look or sound nervous.

"Thank you, I'll check to see if your party is available. One moment please." Areesa tapped her feet and hummed to herself. Her heart was beating hard and loud and her uniform felt like it was weighing her down. She held the phone firmly and pressed it solidly against her ear, so close that it sounded hollow, like a seashell whispering in her ear.

"What if she doesn't know me or my Mom? But why would my own mother set me up to look stupid? Come on, come on . . ." she mumbled.

"I'll connect you to your party. Thank you for using AT&T."

"Hello," the mature voice echoed through the phone.

"Hello," Areesa nervously responded.

"Yes, can I help you?" Addie asked.

"Umm, yes . . . I don't know. I think so. Do you know anyone by the name Davis?"

"No, I don't. Maybe you have the wrong number young lady."

"What about, Charles and Ginny?"

"Ginny?" Addie asked with caution, as she squinted her eyes.

It took Areesa by surprise that someone outside of Jersey, knew her parents. They always told her there were no friends or family outside the three of them.

"Yes. She's my Mom. I'm Areesa."

"Areesa. Ginny's child," Addie acknowledged, trying to clear her thoughts.

"Yes. Charles and Ginny are my parents."

"They're dead aren't they?" Addie asked with her eyes closed and her left hand clinched over her heart the way she did over twenty-two years ago. Areesa didn't know what to say. Her confusion increased and her heart raced faster.

"Where are you child?"

"First of all how do you know my parents?"

"Ariisa, are you here in Denver? It would be better if we talked in person."

"Talk in person. Lady I don't even know you," she said, wiping her tears away, trying to keep her voice from cracking, "I'm only calling because of a promise I made to my Mom. Your name seemed to have meaning to her before she ..." Areesa was breathing heavy and her legs felt wobbly, "Yes, they're dead. So my promise has been kept. Good-bye."

"No, no, no! Don't hang up, please. I know this is difficult for you, I've lost a brother and a best friend."

"A best friend? A brother? Lady my Mom didn't have a best friend and my Dad didn't have a sister. They would have told me if they did."

"Yes, child they did. Twenty-two years ago, they lived right here in Denver. Your mother and I went to school together. We were best friends. I introduced her to my brother, your Dad," Addie said, composed as she possibly could be. Because she didn't want Areesa to know how unprepared she was to receive a call from her. "Yes. He was my brother, my Charlie. Ariisa, did they tell you anything about what happened to them?"

"Tell me anything? Anything like what? And my name is A-rees-a. My Mom just said to call you and you would tell me. So now, I know."

"I need to talk with you, about them, their life here ..."

"I can't deal with this. I can't believe they would keep this from me?"

"Let me come ... get you and we'll talk. I'll answer all of your questions."

"What's so important that you can't tell me over the phone? Tell me now, or never. I'm not in the market for relatives so it doesn't matter to me anyway."

"Ariisa . . . Areesa, please, this is not the way, I know your mother and Charlie wouldn't want you behaving . . ." Areesa interrupted Addie, extremely angered by her presumption of how her parents would expect her to behave. "Hold-up Lady, I don't even know you! and who are you to tell me how to act? I've never spoken to you before and from what I gather my Mom and Dad haven't spoken to you in over twenty-two years. Who are you, to be telling me, how to act? You don't know them, anymore, and you certainly don't know me."

"But you're wrong. Your Mother and Charlie meant everything to me. I loved them. I am saddened that I was unable to be there for them when they needed . . ."

"Needed what? Anyway, what's so important that you can't tell me over the phone? Like I said, tell me now or never tell me, it doesn't matter to me one way or the other."

"No, no child. It's just that the situation is not black and white the way you want it to be. There's much that lies ahead of you and I know your Mother and Charlie would want me to . . . Ariisa. Areesa, please this is not the way I know your mother and Charlie . . . your Dad would want you to see me."

"Hey Lady, first of all why do you keep saying my Mother and Charlie? They're my parents. I've never called him Charlie. I call him Dad. Ariisa, Charlie, what is with you," Areesa said annoyed.

"Oh, I see. They never told you. Ok." Addie took a deep breath and released it. "I can not speak to you any further about this over the phone. Where are you?"

"Hey Davis, what's wrong? You're kinda loud over here for a Private," Tiffoni said placing her hand on her shoulder. Areesa muffled the phone in her shirt, and "Shhhed," Tiffoni.

"Are you still there? Areesa are you still there?" Addie yelled into the phone.

"Areesa who are you talking to? Why are you crying? What's wrong?" Tiffoni questioned. Areesa snatched away from her and shhhed her again.

"I have to go. You can keep whatever you have to say to yourself."

"Areesa you don't understand. Charlie is not your Dad," Addie blurted out. "I know your Mom didn't want you to find out this way," she continued, attempting damage control, "this is why she wanted you to contact me. There's so much more I need to tell you, but I can not do this over the phone, not this way. I must see you. Your past is more than you can imagine. Please let me help you? I love all three of you. Not one day has gone by that I haven't thought or prayed for all of you. And now, they're dead. I need you too Areesa, to tell me who they were, how they made it. I need to know if they found any kind of peace in their lives?"

"Not-my-father?" Areesa said more for her own ears than to Addie.

"I didn't intend for you to hear it this way. Please know that Areesa, but you're so angry, I just . . ."

"Not-my-father. Oh, my God, I can't do this anymore. I just can't do this anymore." Areesa collapsed into the arms of Drill Sergeant Patterson. Tiffoni picked up the phone screaming, "Who is this? What have you done?"

Addie abruptly hung up the phone without responding to Tiffoni's demands, and immediately dialed a number. A man answered. "I need your help. I have to find someone. I don't know much, only her assumed name, Areesa. I think it's spelled A-r-i, no, e-e-s-a, last name is Davis. I think. I can't be certain right now. I heard this information in the background of a conversation on the phone. Oh, yes something else, Private. She called her Private. Please get back to me as soon as you have anything." Addie rolled her diamond earring around on her fingertips as she replaced the phone in its cradle. Addie felt emotionally exhausted and terrified by what had taken place. "I never thought it would come to this, Lord. Make a way for me to get to her."

. . . IN THE MEAN TIME

Military Medics took Areesa out of the PX on a stretcher, with Tiffoni and Drill Sergeant A. Patterson by her side. "Areesa, it's going to be ok, I'm right here. I promise I won't leave you," she said as the medics load Areesa into the back of the ambulance. Sergeant Patterson didn't say anything to her. He sat quietly, with his hands clasped together, resting on top of his drill sergeant hat. She held his face in her eyes, he didn't look away. He looked huge in the cramped space of the ambulance. She turned towards Tiffoni without acknowledging his presence, but she felt safe knowing he was there. Areesa smiled at her, then she closed her eyes. "Stryker, what happened?" Sergeant Patterson questioned, not in his usual husky tone, but in a whisper.

"I don't know. I don't know."

LATER THAT NIGHT . . .

Areesa was taken to the Post Hospital Emergency Room for observation. Her vision was blurry and she still felt disoriented when she came to. A nurse was in the room.

"Hello young Lady, how are you feelin'?" she asked as she wrote on her chart.

"OK," Areesa said softly.

"Do you know where you are?"

"I hope in a hospital."

"Well thank God for miracles, huh. Do you know what day it is," the nurse continued.

"Is my Buddy here?"

"Yes, and what day is it?"

"Not my birthday," Areesa said jokingly.

"A sense of humor is a good sign. Some people are outside waiting for you. Would you like to see them?"

"How long have I been here?"

"About four hours. We sedated you once you arrived. You were distressed and we needed you to relax." She said taking Areesa's pulse, "You can get dressed while I get a release authorization from the attending physician." The nurse left the room and Tiffoni simultaneously entered the room. Areesa was happy to see her, but she was also expecting to see Sergeant Patterson come in behind her.

"He left," Tiffoni said, tinkering with the vitals monitor. Areesa didn't respond. She turned her head away from Tiffoni trying to hide her disappointment.

"He just left, Areesa. He sat out there with me for the entire time. He left a few times to check in. Other than that, he was right here. He doesn't talk much. I don't see what you see in him," Tiffoni concluded.

"Tiffoni, there you go. Reading into things. I'm sure he would have been here for any one of us."

"Yea right. I thought the nurse said you were feeling better, and not delusional anymore."

"He stayed the whole time? Why didn't he come in to see me?" Areesa thought to herself.

"Girl, you had me scared. You were yelling and crying. And whoever was on the phone hung up without asking if you were alright. What happened? Who were you talking to?"

"I don't want to talk about it right now." Tiffoni saw that familiar sadness come back on her face. Tiffoni knew, when Areesa was ready to talk, she'd be there to listen. She didn't push the subject any further. She got Areesa's BDUs off the chair and handed them to her.

"Do you think we'll be getting dropped for any push-ups? Could they possibly hold sympathy, no empathy in their bottomless souls, cause you know Buddy, when you're sick, I'm sick. So if you don't get down, I don't get down," Tiffoni said. Areesa laughed shaking her head side to side.

"Tiffoni you're always one step ahead of the game."

Areesa and Tiffoni waited for the troop shuttle bus to take them back to their training sight. "He could've waited and given us a ride. I know he has a nice ride. I think it's that black navigator," Tiffoni said, looking down the street for the bus.

"Here it comes. The big green giant," Areesa said pointing at the long school bus that was now army green. They got on the bus and four other soldiers from Bravo 1-5, the other platoon on the other end of the hall, were taking up the last four remaining seats by stretching their legs across them. When they saw them get on the bus, they didn't move their feet. Tiffoni and Areesa walked towards the remaining seat in the back of the bus. This agitated Tiffoni because she wanted to sit by herself. It bothered Areesa too, but not as much as it did Tiffoni, because she really disliked these particular females.

"Ok, we can tell when we're not wanted," Tiffoni said loudly to Areesa.

"Don't start Tiffoni. They're already tripping back at the barracks, we don't need no incidents. I'm not feeling good and I'd hate to have to get off this bus," Areesa said flopping onto the empty seat and pulling Tiffoni down with her.

A click of four soldiers, Gill, Yates, Simmons, and Goodman, began harassing Areesa the day after she and Tiffoni were dropped to do push-ups by Drill Sergeant Patterson. Ever since that day these soldiers were always talking to other soldiers about Areesa, how she pretends to be so helpless and innocent. The second round of antagonistic posturing began when Areesa was chosen, along with several other soldiers, for leadership positions because of their prior college background. When Areesa joined the Army, her rank was Private First Class (PFC), as a result of attending college for two years. As squad leader, she and the others delivered orders from the Drill Sergeants to their perspective platoons. They were often charged with developing duty roosters for cleaning details, Charge of Quarters (CQ) duties, and KP (kitchen patrol). Earlier in the week, Drill Sergeant West called Goodman and Gill in his office for disobeying Areesa's order not to use the pay phone during duty hours. Soon after their chastisement, the same privates harassed Areesa in the latrine shower and Tiffoni came to her rescue. Gill especially disliked Areesa. So much so that she watched every encounter, interaction, spoken and unspoken word between Drill Sergeant Patterson and Areesa. She was the first to say Drill Sergeant Patterson was giving Areesa special treatment.

Gill's aggressions towards Areesa was so deep that any one who laughed with Areesa, supported her and spoke of her in a positive way, Gill disliked them. She would make threats to show Areesa up for who she really was, a get over who wanted the world to bow down to her. During the fourth week of

Basic Training, Gill started a rumor that Areesa could expect a blanket party, (wrapping her in a blanket, then beating her up), any night. When Tiffoni heard about what they were planning to do, she stepped to Gill whenever the opportunity presented its self. The word was out. Nothing was going to happen to Areesa as long as she was there! Tiffoni didn't mind, because she loathed females like Gill. Tiffoni believed in brains getting you through life, not your position as a woman or brawn, which Gill had a lot of the latter. To say the least she was a big girl, tall, and stocky. Tiffoni always asked her at the most embarrassing times if she needed to be on a "big girl" program and not in the Army. Areesa, on the other hand simply took the harassment to avoid any intervention from Drill Sergeant Patterson, who seemed to always end up dogging her the most for being in the situation. He often said, "I expect more from a PFC." Everyone thought she was getting special treatment from him, but she felt differently. Over, and over again she felt ambivalent when it came to her feelings about him. She admitted to herself that she liked him, but she was fully aware of his pride and respect for his responsibility and role as a Drill Sergeant. She knew by the way he carried himself, that being a Drill Sergeant had great meaning to him. Unlike some of the other Drills, he would never cross the line of loosing his bearings by fraternizing with her or anyone else. So, she kept her feelings, concerning him, to herself. No one would believe her anyway that nothing, *nothing* was going on between them. Sometimes she would get mad at Tiffoni for the way she came off, subtly implying or inquiring if there was something going on. No matter what she said, Tiffoni didn't believe her when she would say she was as curious about him as the others. Especially, about his name, but she knew it was just as well that she didn't know what the "A" stood for either.

"Why do you take so much trash from them? Especially Gill. I'd love to just slap her in her face," Tiffoni whispered to Areesa while rolling her eyes at Gill. "Like I said, Tiffoni, I don't feel good and I'm not up to mediating a fight between you and Gill. So cool it for the last time."

"What's up Gill?" Tiffoni said, ignoring Areesa, "You know you better show up back at the barracks, or I'm going to report you AWOL (Absent With Out Leave)," Tiffoni said. Areesa dropped her head because she knew it was on. She tried putting her hand over Tiffoni's mouth, but Tiffoni snatched her hand away and looked at Areesa with contempt. "This is the perfect time for payback about the latrine," Tiffoni said. Gill tried standing up on the bus, but it bounced her back into her seat. The bus driver looked at them through his rear mirror, but he didn't say anything. Areesa grabbed at Tiffoni's hand and pulled her back down in the seat with the help of gravity and a sharp turn. Areesa got on her knees in her seat, with her hand held up in a stopping motion. "Check this out, we've been In a private war since day one. Us against the four of you so let's end it here and now," Areesa's heart was pounding fast, but she pressed on with her challenge.

"Yea that's what I'm talking about. Let's do *it* right here while we're still near the hospital," Tiffoni shouted at Gill.

"You're just asking for it Stryker. Yea let's do it right here on the bus," Gill said moving closer to Tiffoni and Areesa.

"No!" Areesa shouted, "I've got something better. How about out on the field tomorrow during our final PT test."

"Our PT test, girl-friend what you talking about?"

"On the field. The best two of you," she firmly said pointing at each of them, "against Tiffoni and me. The best scores win. Better yet, the best-combined scores win. *Losers* pick up the winners' slack in the barracks until we leave."

"What?"

"Come on Gill, put your mouth where your heart is, where it really counts. Us, fighting on this bus is not going to solve anything except get us all a one-way ticket back to the block. But good competition. Who can get in trouble for some good old wholesome competition? Losers have to do the winner's final details, buffing, cleaning, mopping, and *we* will even add in uniforms as the icing. Losers have to starch all the winners' uniforms, spit shine all their boots, pack up their bags and carry them down to the bus when it's time to leave. How 'bout it Gill?" They were all paused, only the bus-humming engine could be heard.

"You trippin' Davis, but yea. I'm down. Me and Yates, we're gonna smoke you, and yo' girl." Tiffoni's body went limp in the seat and she covered her face with her hands and mumbled, "Areesa, PT?"

"Exactly. Gill thinks you can't do it because you were recycled for PT. But we know differently, right?"

"We're going to destroy 'em," she said, laughing as she sat up looking at the competition, "Do you know who we are?" Tiffoni asked rhetorically. "You two are looking at the push-up queens and the best runners in A-1-5." Areesa and Tiffoni high-fived each other, "You're through. You-are-through. I like my uniform crisply starched and I want to see your monkey-dog face, in my boots, Gill."

"Tiffoni! that's enough," Areesa said.

"That's it! I'm gonna get you Stryker," Gill said jumping from her seat. Areesa grabbed Tiffoni and Yates grabbed Gill.

"Save it for the field ladies," Areesa said as the bus stopped at their end of the barracks.

"Yea, save your strength, because you, are going to need it," Tiffoni said, nick-picking as Areesa pushed her off the bus. Tiffoni turned quickly and stepped onto the bus again, "It's on you witches. It's on," she said pointing her finger like a gun at them. Gill jumped up to catch her, but the doors slammed and the bus pulled away as she slapped the window at Tiffoni's face.

"You just had to do it, didn't you Tiffoni?"

"Yea, I did."

"You better hope I'm feeling well by tomorrow or you're going to do everything!"

"What? Why are you going out like that?" Tiffoni asked. Areesa stopped in her tracks without looking at Tiffoni, "I didn't know people with money could talk so much trash."

"What do you think I use the money for? To cover what my butt can't handle," she said slapping Areesa on the back as she raced pass her crossing the street and entering the barracks.

"Rich people. I had no idea."

the challenge

"Rise and shine Josephines! Get up! Get your lazy-behinds out of my bunks," Drill Sergeant West yelled, randomly banging his pistol belt against beds and lockers.

"Great, yours truly," Tiffoni said rolling off her bunk.

Sergeant West continued his daily yelling ritual as he passed Areesa's bed, but he didn't say anything about her still laying there.

"Stryker get your Buddy up," he ordered. "Ok this is the outlook for today. Final PT test at 1600 hours and more drill and ceremony practice. Yea, yea that's right more drill and ceremony. So stop your moaning, it's not over until I say it's over. Those of you who've qualified with your weapon, who are up to speed on drills and ceremonies, *with-out-getting-out-of-step*," he emphasized, "and can follow orders, will continue to drive on. Your next mission at hand is your final PT test. I can't hear yooou."

"MORE P-T SERGEANT, MORE P-T. WE LIKE IT. WE LOVE IT. WE WANT MORE OF IT. DRIVE ON DRILL SERGEANT, DRIVE ON!" Alpha 1-5's voices roared.

"All right. Friday is Graduation. Stop smiling. You're not out of my house yet. Two days is still enough time to separate the girls from the soldiers," he said, scanning the Bay for unbelievers. Silence entered the room. They realized he was serious, because Basic Training was not over until you were dragging your worn, torn, over stimulated body, onto a bus with your orders in your hand. They understood that the PT test was about teamwork if they wanted everyone in their platoon to make it because everyone had to pull together and draw from the Drill Sergeants and fellow platoon members' cheering, to run faster and not give up. They all knew, if you failed PT, you would have to stay and join another cycle of trainees like Tiffoni had to do. Every eye and ear was on him waiting for his next block of instructions. "There is still work to get done Josephines, remember that. Pictures in your Class A Uniform, (the Army Dress Green), will be taken today beginning at 0-9-30 hours. Only wear the top portion of your uniform. You can wear moderate make-up. Don't fall-out looking like a make-up queen for a commercial, that is if you don't want to be embarrassed. Do I lie Carlyle?"

"No DRILL SERGEANT."

"So take me and Carlyle's advice and don't try me." Everyone laughed, except the females who were always whining about their lost privilege to wear make-up during Basic. The Drill Sergeants' advice was, "Make-up clogs pores. Wearing it draws bugs. If having bugs swarming around your head, in your eyes, up your nose don't irritate you, then the dirt from low crawling in sand, mud, or wood bark mixing with your foundation will. If that don't bother you maybe sweat mixing in with your mascara burning your eyes out after a five mile road march every other week will. Either way, in the end, you will have an ugly matted look that causes rashes and pimples, if you so chose, to wear make-up during training." With that said, most didn't wear make-up. The others would come in after training put on make-up, hang out in the latrine, then wash it off before lights out, time to go to bed. The Army made people do strange things. Non-smokers became smokers. Non-drinkers became big-time drinkers. Cursors, cursed more and those who didn't eventually did. The profane became vulgar, and the innocent became impure. The weak became stronger, or fell by the waist side and the prideful fell at the command of a drill sergeant. No one was left unchanged by the traditional ceremonious lures of Basic Training.

"Myself, and Drill Sergeant Patterson will march the platoon over to Delta Hall for final graduation practice," they all moaned and groaned about more practicing. "Oh stop it. If yall focus, and stop griping Josephines, you wouldn't have to get out there everyday. I have everyone's orders for their next assignment. No!" he said not giving anyone a chance to ask questions, "Wait until after lunch. I'll give them to you then. Now, last, but not least. Those of you, and you know who you are, who have to travel the trail again, pack your duffel bags, strip my bunks, clean my lockers, turn in my linen, and get on your way. I do wish you well in your new Basic Training Company."

"The man knows no shame," Tiffoni bent over and whispered into Areesa's ear, making her laugh.

"Formation is at 0-7-30 hours. BDUs, is the uniform for today. Fonte, what's your weapon?" Sergeant West asked, selecting Privates at random to see and hear what they knew. Standing quickly, coming to attention she responded, "M-16, magazine feed, air cooled, gas operated, semi or fully automatic weapon, fired from the hip or shoulder position, Drill Sergeant," she said in one-breath.

"Young, who is in your chain of command?"

"Squad Leader- PFC Pike, Drill Sergeants- Sergeant First Class West and Staff Sergeant Patterson, 1st Sergeant Curry, and Company Commander-Captain Strouble, Drill Sergeant," she sounded off like a high-tech computerized android, not breaking the position of attention.

"I like that, I like that," he commended her. Tiffoni leaned over and whispered in Areesa's ear, hoping to keep a smile on her face, "He would like a response that sounds as whined up as he is." Areesa poked Tiffoni in the side. She got up off her bed and gave Tiffoni a hug. Drill Sergeant West caught a glimpse of their moment and decided to get around to Alpha 1-5's favorite buddies. If they weren't squared away they knew the deal, DROP into the front leaning rest position. "Stryker," he bellowed.

"I knew it," Tiffoni said throwing both her hands up in the air.

"What is your First General Order?"

"I will guard everything within the limits of my post, and quit my post only when properly relived, Drill Sergeannnt!" Tiffoni responded.

"Yea, right Tiffoni," someone yelled out, and the Bay filled with laughter, because everyone knew she would abandon her post at any given moment for no reason, other than she wanted to. Sergeant West blew off her antics and Areesa cracked up laughing.

"Davis!" Areesa jumped, "Ivy, Walker, and Hasan on your feet and fall-in. On my command execute: "Right face," they moved in perfect harmony. "About face." With a snap they executed his command. "Mark-time march." They began to march in place on time and in step. "Squad halt." One, two, without flinching or swaying they stopped and sounded off, "ROCK STEA-DY ALPHA! ROCK STEA-DY.

"Squared away, Josephines. Looking like real soldiers. Now lets get busy," he said.

Drill Sergeant West was particularly proud of the soldiers in this cycle. He and Sergeant Patterson had a high percent of soldiers who were; discharged for misconduct or failure to comply; became ill or broke something and had to be medically discharged; became pregnant; went AWOL; or couldn't pass the PT test last cycle. This cycle they were going to graduate thirty-three out of thirty-five a huge improvement. "Davis, report to my office in fifteen minutes," Drill Sergeant West said, leaving the Bay on his last command.

Back in his office, he began shuffling the papers around on his desk. Sergeant Patterson rushed into the office, wearing gray gym shorts and a matching T-shirt with the logo Go Alpha 1-5 on the back of his shirt, and US Army written in black letters across his chest. He opened the locker, marked SSG (Staff Sergeant), A. Patterson and took out a pressed BDU uniform, spit-shined boots and his Smoky the Bear Drill Sergeant hat. With his boots and uniform in hand he turned and was about to walk out the door when he decided to ask Sergeant West what he was looking for on his usually messy desk. "If you kept that table top clean you wouldn't have these problems everyday Serg," he said laughing at the familiar event he witnessed every day since he was hooked-up with Sergeant West. He dropped his things on the sofa to give a helping hand.

"Good gracious, where is it?"

"How do you do this, man?"

"Yea, yea, yea. Just save it. I had an emergency message for Davis."

"Davis? From who?" Sergeant Patterson asked, going from a smile to a frown.

"Hey be cool man," Sergeant West said, disapproving of his comrade's concern for her.

"Sure. So who left the message?" Sergeant Patterson asked again, ignoring Sergeant West's warning.

"Patterson!" Sergeant West said slamming his hands on his messy desk. "These Privates come in here every eight weeks. Within that period, we have one mission, to turn these Josephines into soldiers. Prepare them for leadership as NCOs (Non-Commission Officers) capable of leading during a crisis. We haven't the time or God's power to concern ourselves with every aspect of their personal lives when it doesn't affect our mission. So, get with the program man. No Private is worth ten years time with Uncle Sam. No Private is worth throwing your career and future away for," he paused, lowering his voice, "You know Uncle Sam doesn't pat you on the back and send you on your way for fraternizing with new recruits - you can lose everything! Rank, money, retirement, and end up with jail time. Think my man about what you're doing. Think with your head and not from where most men make choices from and you know what I'm saying."

Sergeant Patterson slumped onto the sofa on top of his uniform and boots. He grabbed a boot and threw it across the room. He placed his hands over his face. Slowly he pulled them downward releasing a deep groan. His eyes gazed at the ceiling as if a solution was going to fall down on him. He took another deep breath and released it. He knew the tension between him and Sergeant West was going to cause a conflict based on how he handled the situation with Areesa.

West did think Patterson was harder on Areesa than the other Josephines. Though West saw how Patterson was responding to Areesa, the rumor mill was she hated him that's why whenever she saw him coming, she would go the other direction to avoid him, and Sergeant Patterson knew he would never admit to anyone that he was concerned about her more than he should be. In this moment Sergeant Patterson accepted the fact that whatever was controlling her was now controlling him, and he knew he couldn't tell Sergeant West what he was feeling.

KNOCK * KNOCK

"Yea?"

"Private Davis request permission to enter?"

"What's the way, Davis?" Sergeant West asked.

"Alpha 1-5 all the way!" she yelled.

"Enter." She stepped into the office unaware of Drill Sergeant Patterson sitting on the sofa. The look on Sergeant West's face made her feel uneasy. She traced over his face then she focused in on the wall where all of his awards and certificates hung, to a portrait of his family to a wooden coat hanger, down to a file cabinet to Drill Sergeant A. Patterson sitting on the sofa. "Drill Sergeant Patterson, I'm sorry, I didn't mean to interrupt." It was obvious to her that she had walked in on something. Drill Sergeant West sighed and placed the yellow paper with a message on it face down on the corner of his desk as he left them in the office. Drill Sergeant Patterson remained seated until he heard the office door close. He got up and retrieved the message. He unfolded it, read it and replaced it on the desk, while Areesa remained at attention, looking straightforward at the awards on the wall. "At ease. Please turn and face me, Areesa," he said. She continued to stand perfectly still. She was afraid to face him. She closed her eyes and told herself to relax then she turned to face him after several deep breaths. He looked into her brown eyes, and dropped his head. Her eyes were captivating. The first time he encountered her, that's what he noticed first. "Do you want to sit?" he asked.

"No Drill Sergeant." He handed her the yellow message slip. It read: Call Addie Meaks ASAP #303-555-1493. Areesa was shaken by Addie's ability to find her. She immediately wondered if the Drill Sergeants had spoken with her. What had she told them? Areesa panicked inside. Her breathing was burdened, her chest was clearly rising up and down, her eyes were watery and her body shook on the inside. What Addie may have told them frightened her. She didn't want anyone to know her secret. She felt obligated to guard the secret her parents passionately guarded while they were alive. What they were keeping from her didn't matter. She urged her inner-self to hang on. "Is there anything you'd like to talk about?" Sergeant Patterson asked. She shook her head no, licking then biting her bottom lip. She looked at him and she didn't withdraw her stare. His hair was in little wavy curls caused by his sweating from doing PT. His flexed muscles and the darkness of his damp skin made Areesa more than before, aware of his physical presence. He stood towering over her. Perspiration was around the neck of his T-shirt, under his armpits and around his waist. She looked away trying to conceal her unquestionable feelings for him. She felt him take her hands into his. Her eyes widen and she gazed into his dark eyes, responding to his touch like she was where she always belonged. In that moment, instantly, all of who she was stood there, hand in hand, with a man who had shown her compassion at all the right times, as if he was reading her mind, knowing when to push her and when to encourage her. She didn't want to deny her feelings for him any more. She wanted him to take her in his arms and hold her in the safety of them, so she could feel all that he knew and understood about the world, that a few months ago turned its back on her. They were captured in a moment that came into conflict with time and place.

"If you need to talk Areesa, I'm here . . . for you. I want you to know that a lot of rumors are circulating about us," he said maintaining his hold on her hands, "just remember two days from now you'll be gone. So hang in there. Let them talk, because we know," he uttered in a whisper into the thickness of her hair. She released herself to the moment, and her head gently went forward and rested in the center of his chest. She thought he was going to swoop her up into his arms. She wanted him to. She needed a distraction from the anticipation of kissing him, she glanced at his locker, SSG A. Patterson, she wondered if this was the day she'd learn what his first name was.

"Areesa the time will come, when it will be ok to express what we feel. For now, the place doesn't permit," he reluctantly, but firmly said. She stepped back and snatched her hands from his. Drill Sergeant Patterson diverted his eyes from hers. "I have to get dressed and ready for formation. You can return to your details."

She was stunned and unable to utter any words. She replayed the seconds prior to his order in her mind over and over, and over. She thought, "Have I read too much into this?" She couldn't believe it, his sudden change of heart. "He's always coming on to me like I mean something to him. And then, and then, he just turns me away like a, Private, a Josephine," her thoughts taunted her, reminding her of her foolishness. She turned and rushed out of the office as quickly as she could. She didn't want him to see her crying. Once on the other side of the door, without warning, one lonely tear fell from her eye, reminding her of how she felt.

She put her hands over her mouth and moaned, "What is happening to me? Nothing seems real or right anymore." She wiped her moistened face with her sleeve and composed herself. She realized how tired she was of everyone supposing to know what was good for her. She was tired of always being out of control of her feelings. She knew it had to stop! Outraged she said, "Drill Sergeant Patterson, Private Davis request permission to leave," to his photo hanging on the hall wall in front of her. She pushed her body off the wall and did what the Drill Sergeant ordered, she returned to her duties.

. . . the challenge begins

"Are you OK?"

"What is it Tiffoni?" she asked through clinched teeth?

"You're tripping."

"Oh, am I. How?" she said as she stretched her long legs for the final part of the PT test.

"We're supposed to compete against them, not each other, Areesa," Tiffoni said standing over her, with the sun beaming over her shoulder into Areesa's face.

"What difference does it make? As long as we're not the ones carrying the duffel bags."

"Yea OK," Tiffoni responded as she walked away. "Does this have anything to do with what Sergeant West called you out for? I know you were in the office with Sergeant P. Is everything cool? I'm here for you if you need to talk."

"Why does everybody want me to talk! Talk about what? What is it you wanna hear? The details about my dead parents, or why I'm in the Army? What is it? No, let me guess! Am I, or aren't I having a thing, or something with Sergeant Patterson! The answer is actually none of your business. Let's just finish this stupid race so I can get away from this place, these people, to include all of you who have nothing better to do than figure out what's wrong with Areesa Davis."

"Ok Areesa, I get the point. I'm just concerned about Ms. *Secretive* Areesa Davis, but you know, in spite of that, I thought you were my buddy."

"If one more person tells me about genuine concern I swear I'm going to kill 'em."

"Hey, stay mad. We're winning," Tiffoni said walking away, hurt, but covering it up with sarcasm, as always.

"Tiffoni," Areesa called after her, but Tiffoni ignored her. Areesa hit the ground with her fist. Gill walked by and kicked dirt on her. Areesa jumped to her feet with her fist clinched.

"Gill this is not the day you want to be messing with me."

the challenge builds . . .

"You heard?" Sergeant West asked Sergeant Patterson giving him his stopwatch for the two-mile run.

"Yea."

"What are the scores?"

"I just checked with Shubert and Kirkland. We got'em by fifty points. Gill and Yates can still smoke Davis and Stryker on the run."

"And that ain't happenin'. Davis can run. She could be doing better. They should be running away with this. You can tell she got at-ti-tude about something. I wonder what?" Sergeant West said looking over his shoulder at Sergeant Patterson as they walked towards their soldiers scattered about doing stretching exercises.

"Cut me some slack. You're the one who wanted in on the bet along with Shubert and Kirkland. So save your leadership drama for somebody else."

The Drill Sergeants decided to get in on the bet after hearing about it through the barracks rumor mill because competition like this builds "Esprit De Corps" among the platoons. Sergeant West, the proud leader that he was, knew Davis and Stryker had become well rounded Privates. This was an easy kill as far as he was concerned. For this cycle to end whipping the rival platoon, would build confidence throughout the entire Alpha 1-5 platoon and staff, including the Drill Sergeants. Knowing this, he went over to the other platoon to egg on Gill and Yate's Drill Sergeants Shubert and Kirkland into the same deal. Losing Drill Sergeants had to close down the training site and arrive back early to receive the next cycle.

Sergeant Patterson, on the other hand was concerned about Areesa's behavior. He knew she was hurting inside. When he gave her the message from Addie, he saw how shocked she was to hear from her. This gave way to his conclusion that there was more at stake than what Areesa wanted anyone to know. He understood the importance of his career and he still felt drawn to her. He knew she was running off emotions and not sound reasoning. He thought Addie was possibly her biological mother, based on the night out on the terrace. That was as far as he had gotten in trying to figure out what was going on with her. What ever her secret was she was hiding it at all cost. Though he couldn't explain why, he wanted to help her through it as much as he could, but she wasn't having it, especially from him. So he decided to play amateur detective, without Sergeant West's approval. He began by going through her file. He found no point of contact for her except a woman named Mills, who was listed as a family friend. Her background revealed a lot of moving around and of course, the death certificate for both her parents was in there too. He found out that her home of record was New Jersey. He wondered why someone would call her from Denver, Colorado, because none of her previous addresses was in Denver. No siblings, aunts, uncles, cousins, just a family friend was listed.

He watched her stretching. He remembered how she was when he first encountered her. He was proud of the growth she had made because he would've never imagined her challenging someone to a test, let alone the most challenging test in Basic Training, the PT test.

The two Drill Sergeants where standing near the starting line for the run, laughing about always dropping Areesa and Tiffoni.

"I knew they'd take the push-ups," Sergeant West said, "Who'd have known dropping them would pay off like this," they both laughed.

"I know man. Every time I saw one, I knew the other had to be close by. I'd just say drop. You'd either see or hear the other one grunt or call the other one's name."

"Yea. Into-the-front-leaning-rest-position! My arms were beginning to get sore just from droppin' em all the time."

"Cause if those Josephines had got into a fight on that bus, I tell you what, all of 'em would be sitting on the block right now. Fellas, come on over. We wanna see your sad faces after our best runner smokes what you two are trying to pass off as soldiers," Sergeant West bragged.

"Hey Serg, Gill can run too."

Sergeant Patterson watched Areesa, pace and stretch. Her hands were on her hips as she quickly kicked her legs out constantly moving and twisting her entire body to loosen up, as the wind tossed her loose hair. He realized for the first time that he had never seen her hair down, because Army regulations mandated that females' hair be above the collar, but during PT they were authorized to ware it down. Her hair was always in a ponytail or in two cornrows around her head. Her slender five feet, six inch frame shook and wiggled as she continued to loosen up. She was etched in his mind, but he knew where they were would never permit him to share his feelings. He knew he could never betray his Drill Sergeant Creed. Holding her hands made him realize feelings, he didn't want to feel or deal with in the environment. In spite of his good sense, the feelings were real and steadily growing. "Beautiful," he whispered as she walked to the starting line.

"What did you say, Patterson?" He didn't respond, but kept walking to the starting line where Areesa and about one hundred other soldiers were waiting to start the final leg of their PT test. At the sight of Drill Sergeant Patterson coming towards her, Areesa grew angry. She didn't feel embarrassed about what happened anymore, just humiliated for thinking he wanted to kiss her. She vowed no one would see her vulnerable like that again. Tiffoni watched their reaction towards each other. She shook her head. They were pitiful as far as she was concerned.

"They're tripping," Tiffoni thought as Gill shoved her.

"Your girl ain't gonna be no good to you. She's too love sick," Gill said.

"Go!" one of the Drill Sergeants yelled out, not giving Tiffoni the opportunity to confront Gill.

… the challenge belongs

Gill jumped out ahead of Tiffoni. Yates was neck and neck with Tiffoni, and Areesa was ahead of them all, which is what everyone expected. Gill knew she had to keep her pace close, if she had any hope of beating Areesa

53

or gaining points that could still give her and Yates a small, but sweet victory. Areesa's slender frame encased all the attributes of a good runner. She started out running at a consistent pace and tenacious mind set while controlling her breathing. She had no idea why she liked running. She just did. "You run like you're running from something inside your head," Tiffoni once told her.

Areesa quickened her pace, as she remembered the conversation she had with Tiffoni before the PT test began. "Yea, today I'm running. Running from being me," she said as she exhaled and drew another dose of air into her lungs. As she ran pass the starting line the first time, Sergeant West yelled out her time to urge her on, but she ignored him and all the "Go Davis, Go," chanting as she passed by. She only focused on the vibration of each of her feet rhythmic strides, striking the earth. A parentless child, an illegitimate child. NOT YOUR Dad, NOT YOUR Dad, echoed in her head, not the cheers. Sergeant Patterson's heart quickened as she zoomed passed him on her second lap. He knew she wasn't consciously with them. Gill's effort to stay on her heels was fading fast as more and more distance grew between them. As Areesa ran by on her third lap, the voices cheering her on, was drowned out by the jeering in her head: "NOT YOUR Dad, NOT YOUR Dad. Who are you? Is it true? Your Mom is a liar. Who's your Dad . . . who? Who?" She ran faster, and faster, and faster. Sergeant Patterson was worried she was going to give out before she started her final lap. "Slow down, girl, slow down," he said as she ran past him.

"Go Davis. You can do it. Run, run. You can make it." Areesa's long legs sprinted forth as she pumped arms up and down. Caught up in emotion, ignoring the seasonal weather or the pressure to win, she freely moved through the air, only bound by her thoughts. Then she sensed Gills' approach. In order to get a Go on their PT test they needed to complete four laps (equal to two miles) in under 15 minutes for their age and gender category. Areesa looked over her shoulder to estimate where Gill was, because she was not going to let Gill out run her. She also caught a glimpse of Tiffoni struggling to stay with Yates. Her face was strained, her arms were drooping, her back was slightly bent as she struggled to balance her body and control her breathing. Areesa looked forward and saw Drill Sergeant West out in the street with his stopwatch in one hand, while waving her in with his other hand. Fellow One-fivers were in the street too chanting, "Go Davis, Go." Areesa could see Gill in her left peripheral vision trying to overtake her. "It'll never happen, baby," she taunted at Gill as she stretched her legs out in long energetic strides, crossing the finish line in less than nine minutes and thirty seconds! Sergeant West snapped his stopwatch yelling out her new record for 1st Battalion, over the excitement and jubilation of the crowd and explosive cheering from Drill Sergeant Patterson.

Feeling victorious and pumped up from the exhilaration she gets from running, she didn't forget about her girl, her Buddy. It became apparent that Yates and Tiffoni were in a race of their own, they would be the deciding factor. Yates needed to finish in twelve minutes and Tiffoni needed to finish in eleven minutes and thirty seconds. Surrounded, everyone was patting her on the back or grabbing her hand to shake it, as she pushed through them, looking for Tiffoni. She made her way through as Gill came in, heading straight for her, but she jumped out of the way onto the curb as Gill crossed the line, with not the best time, but still a competitive time. The race was all on Tiffoni. Areesa stepped back down onto the street. She searched several strained faces, until she saw Tiffoni who was in the midst of the remaining runners, only a few paces ahead of Yates. "Run Tiffoni, run. You can do it," Areesa yelled out with her hands around her mouth like a bullhorn. "Stryker! you'd better get here first or you're going to be recycled again," Sergeant Patterson added. Areesa, disapproving, rolled her eyes at him.

"Don't worry about it Tiffoni. You can do it. Run Tiffoni, show 'em all you can do it. You're not recyclable material," she said looking at Sergeant Patterson with contempt in her eyes. Sergeant Patterson smiled. He was glad to hear and see she was no longer in the race for herself. That she had gotten yesterday off her mind and was focusing in on her Buddy's struggle-at-hand. Areesa, still in the street with Sergeant Patterson behind her holding up his stopwatch yelling out Tiffoni's time, knew, if she didn't come in within the next forty seconds they would lose.

Both platoons took over the street yelling out Yates, or Tiffoni's name. Tiffoni heard one voice over all the others, Areesa's voice, a homing device calling her in. "Straighten up Tiffoni and pump, Girl! You'd better pump it up! I'm not playing. Get those legs out there," Areesa said walking towards the finishing line. Drill Sergeant Patterson moved with her, attempting to calmly state Tiffoni's remaining time, "29, 28, 27, 26 …," he said as Areesa continued to approach the finish line. "Look up Tiffoni! Look at me. Now sprint! You can do it! Run Tiffoni, run," she yelled. Everything Areesa told Tiffoni to do, of course Yates did it too. But Areesa didn't care. Areesa was at the line almost squatting with her arms open wide, encouraging Tiffoni to press on. The platoon and Drill Sergeant West continued cheering her on to beat Yates. As the voices wailed behind Areesa, she maintained her outstretched arms focusing in on Tiffoni and she concentrated on Areesa's open arms. She commanded her body to run faster, and faster, and faster. Tiffoni began getting a bigger lead on Yates, and Alpha 1-5 went out of control, but Drill Sergeant Patterson, maintained his calm as he kept his eyes on his stopwatch, "15, 14, 13," he said standing closely behind Areesa.

"Run! Tiffoni run! Run girl. You run girl! You'd better run, come on Foni, bring it on home," Areesa passionately urged her realizing that Tiffoni's time was running out.

"She'd better start sprinting. 11, 10 ..." Sergeant Patterson yelled out over the earsplitting cheering, "9, 8 ... tell her to push. She can do it."

"Push Tiffoni, push. Hurry, hurry, hurry . . .," Areesa said pumping her clinched fist in the air. Tiffoni ran right into Areesa's arms dragging her backwards, they bumped into Sergeant Patterson, and all three of them fell to the ground. Tiffoni and Areesa were in tears, hugging and laughing about their victory.

"You did it Buddy."

"Yea, we did it," Tiffoni said.

"OK, Privates. Can I get up now?" Sergeant Patterson requested with a big smile on his face.

let the whoopla begin

Graduation Day was a long time coming, a constant haul, but they made it, most of them. It also meant that Basic Training was almost over. The *entire* platoon was excited, because they knew graduation morning meant-one day and a wake up, they'd no longer be living in Alpha 1-5 Basic Training Barracks, as Trainees. As much as they wanted this day to come, unexpectedly, a sense of loss was mixed with the excitement they felt.

Alpha 1-5 was not busying about the Bay. Movement was slow and purposeful. Some attentively removed lent from their Army Green Uniforms; others were meticulously pinning polished brass rank in its appropriate place on the lapels and the front of their jackets. Some had their arms inserted in stockings, checking for runs. Some sat on the floor, spit shinning their loafers, while others were selecting post earrings, to match foundations and lipsticks they could now wear. Solemn laughing echoed out, from different areas in the Bay, much unlike the robust burst of laughter that often resounded after Drill Sergeant Jokes. Some were quiet, many had cried at least once, as they readied themselves for the day none of them would ever forget.

THE NEXT MORNING . . .

"You look outstanding Buddy," Tiffoni said proudly.

"You don't look too shabby yourself, Buddy"

"Now, GET-ON-DOWN-BUDDY."

"No-you-get-on-down, Buddy," Areesa said, mocking Drill Sergeant West, who often spoke with long pauses between all of his words. "We did it Tiffoni," Areesa said, nudging Tiffoni's arm as they approached the Bay's double doors. "Come on we better hurry before we miss formation. We don't wanna backslide," Areesa said as she slid back, "to our old ways, always being late for formation. It would be tacky if we went out the way we came in . . ."

"In the front leaning rest positiooon," Tiffoni said, finishing Areesa's sentence. They both automatically got down into the push-up position alternating their positions, so that one was up when the other was down, "Thank you Areesa for conditioning my mind and my body, Private Stryker request permission to recover."

"Recover." In one movement, Tiffoni leaped to their feet, pausing at attention. "Let's go buddy," Tiffoni said extending her hand to Areesa. Areesa took her hand and Tiffoni pulled her up. They momentarily stared at each other.

"Yea, lets go," Areesa said as she placed her right toe behind her left heal, and spun her entire body around in an about-face movement.

"I'm right behind you," Tiffoni said, balancing her cap on her head, and then taking two purposeful steps to stand beside Areesa.

"I made it Mom and Dad. And I'm not alone anymore. I have Tiffoni," she thought as she smiled at Tiffoni.

"Don't forget, my Father will be at the graduation party. I'm excited about you meeting him, Areesa."

"Me too. Is he as snobbish as you are? You know how you rich black folks can be."

"Yea I know how we rich black folks can be," Tiffoni agreed laughing. "He's leaving Denver, as we speak. He'll get here tonight."

"Denver. Denver, Colorado? I didn't know you were from Denver."

"We never talked about it. After all this time and you still don't know me," Tiffoni said jokingly.

"Yea," Areesa said into the mirrored glass on the Bay door as she straighten her cap. She hoped Tiffoni didn't pick up on her surprise. She turned and walked with her head held high and her heart filled with pride, out of the double doors to join her family, Alpha 1-5 for their important day.

"Company. Atten-tion." Two hundred and fifty soldiers snapped into the position of attention. "Right-face. Forwaaard March." The group moved out towards the parade field where family and friends were lining the streets like parade watchers pointing and waving at their soldier. Areesa's eyes roamed through the crowd wanting to see someone out there waving frantically at her, mouthing to her well done with a thumb held high in the sky. She attempted to put her parents' faces on others. She tried finding people who looked like them so she could put on a broad smile and pretend for just a moment they were waving at her. Tiffoni broke rank with her right hand, reached over, and touched Areesa's hand. Neither of them turned their heads from the straightforward position they were required to maintain while marching, they squeezed each other's hand and continued to march forward. Unknowing to Areesa no one was out there for Tiffoni either. They both continued to march and chant the cadence Drill Sergeant West was leading:

(DS= Drill Sergeant / Ts = Trainees)

DS: This is graduation Day
Ts: Drill Sergeant, you know I can't wait
  It's almost time to go home
  Drill Sergeant, you know I can't wait
  Gonna party all night long
  Drill Sergeant, you know I can't wait
  I know you wanna go home
  Yea, I wanna go home

"Company," he commanded, "mark-time march." The soldiers continued to hum the cadence without the lead of the Drill Sergeant while one-two stepping in place waiting for his next command. "Company, halt." The soldier's feet thundered as they stopped in two steps, then they sounded off, loud enough to force some parade watchers to place their hands over their ears, "ROCK STEADY DRILL SERGEANTS, ROCK STEADY." The next command came as an immediate response, "File from the right, MOVE." In a single line, they began filing one after the other into the Post Chapel.

The ceremony began with a brief *job well done* speech by the Battalion Commander. The Post Commander's speech reiterated traditional duties and obligation to country and army and he encouraged them to serve with pride and honor. He also told them how proud they all should feel about their great accomplishment, completing eight weeks of training and becoming highly trained efficient soldiers. He concluded with the most important fact of all, that they were all potential leaders, future Non-commissioned Officers (NCOs), who may someday return as Drill Sergeants themselves to train new young soldiers or lead them in war during a time of crisis for the great country they all served, the United States of America. Areesa, Tiffoni and all the others sat proudly in chapel on a day that turned out to be all they expected.

Next, Commandant's Awards were given for the Best Drill & Ceremony and Most Improved Trainee. The Best of the Fittest Award went to Areesa and she was one of several to receive recognition for academic achievement.

"The Academic Award for highest Grade Point Average (GPA), is awarded to Private Tiffoni Stryker," the Commander announced. Coughs, stirs, and rumbling filled the chapel as Tiffoni stood up. Areesa, shocked, didn't move to let Tiffoni pass by. Tiffoni looked down on her and said, "Areesa. Move."

"Oh, yea, right," she said trying to turn her knees slightly to the right so Tiffoni could pass through, "I didn't know, I thought . . ."

"I know what you thought. Can you move so I can go and get my award," she said.

"Oh, yea. Sure. Congrat . . . ."

"Yea, yea. Yadda, yadda Areesa," she said as she stepped on Areesa's spit shined shoes, and all the others who did not move, as she made her way down the aisle. Areesa shrugged her shoulders, when others looked her way. She wondered if Tiffoni knew she was getting the award. "Probably so," Areesa thought to herself, "but why didn't she mention it, like the Denver, thing?"

On the words of congratulations from the Commander, the new graduates removed their headgear, and tossed the headgear high in the air, simultaneously shouting, "Rock Steady," followed by, Alpha, or Bravo, or Charlie, or Delta or Echo. "Rock Steady," they shouted again as headgear rained down on them, on church pews, and the floor as they leaned over pews and crossed aisles shaking each other's hands and hugging.

"AT EASE!" Sergeant West commanded. Silence filled the chapel. The soldier's eight weeks of training showed by their obedience to his command. Still in place, they waited for his next command. "FALL IN," he said. The soldiers quietly returned to their original places in the chapel. "On my command you will file out, from the front, in a single line into a formation outside in your designated area. Battalion. Attention. Center - face." A long pause, then he said, "Drill Sergeants." The Drill Sergeants entered the aisles and began their leaving the chapel. Drill Sergeant Patterson followed Sergeant West out of the chapel. He glanced at Areesa and smiled. She returned his smile, and Tiffoni made a low gagging sound.

The first two rows of soldiers seated in the front of the chapel, on the left and right side, began filing into the aisle. One at a time, they stepped into the aisle smiling and secretly grabbing at each other's hand. As one row emptied, the next row began to follow the last person from the previous row until all the rows were vacant. The last soldier, the Ceremony Soldier, stopped at the large oak double doors and came to the position of attention. She took four, thirty- inch paces, then stopped at the chapel thresh-hole. Standing on the chapel porch, she did an about-face, then reached for the door's handles. With both her hands firmly holding the handles she pulled the doors towards her body, and stepped backwards closing them. She about-faced once again. Pausing for ten seconds she saluted the Battalion flag, ribbons, and colors as another soldier removed the flag from its holder on the chapel porch. A Drill Sergeant returned the salute to the soldier, as the flag was raised high in the sky. The Drill Sergeant about faced and the soldier holding the flag lowered it down close to his torso and stepped up to the left side of the Drill Sergeant. The Ceremony Soldier stepped up and stood on the right side of the Drill Sergeant. The three stood shoulder to shoulder maintaining the position of attention. Then they stepped out in thirty-inch marching steps to the front of the Battalion formation. Once the ceremony squad was in place, the Command Sergeant Major surrendered a salute to the Battalion Commander. The Commander returned the salute with verbal orders. "Take charge of the soldiers for further ceremonial activities." The Sergeant Major remained at attention, as the Commander dropped his salute, then he right faced and swiftly stepped away from the Battalion formation. The Sergeant Major dropped his salute and about-faced. He stood centered on the formation of Drill Sergeants and platoons of soldiers. He relayed the orders from the Commander. "Take charge of your platoon and march them back to the company area for further ceremonial activities."

Each Platoon Drill Sergeant surrendered a salute to the Sergeant Major. The five senior Drill Sergeants in sync dropped their salutes and about-faced on the command of the Sergeant Major. The Assistant Drill Sergeants took over the directional commands and called cadence for the formation as they marched back to the Barrack's site. Drill Sergeant A. Patterson marched along side the human train with all the other Drill Sergeants and called a poetic cadence to keep the soldiers in step. Two hundred plus men and women voices responded to his lyrical chant:

DS: *Everywhere I go*
    Ts: There's a Drill Sergeant there
When I eat my food
There's a Drill Sergeant there
When I call back home
There's a Drill Sergeant there
When I run PT
There's a Drill Sergeant there
When I wanna be alone
There's a Drill Sergeant there
Drill Sergeant
Drill Sergeant
Won't you leave me alone
Won't you leave me alone
Cause I wanna go home
Cause I wanna go home
Goin' on home
I'm goin' on home
Yea I'm goin' home

the honorable thing

"Areesa, come meet my father," Tiffoni said grabbing her hand, dragging her away from the group she was standing with.

Once again, Tiffoni failed to mention an important fact. Her father was a Colonel. Not any Colonel. But, *the* Colonel Stryker often seen on all the major news broadcast giving briefings from the Pentagon in Arlington. Who had recently been profiled in the Army Times pending his promotion to Brigadier General and his new staff job at the Pentagon. In addition, the Colonel was celebrated throughout the Army, for setting standards for Army-wide policies, and for his leadership positions in elite stateside and overseas commands. He served two tours in Vietnam and held a strategic position during Desert Shield/Storm. Colonel Stryker's distinguished reputation for accomplishing missions, his physical presence to lead, and confident demeanor preceded him wherever he went. His dedication, high achievements, and commentaries while serving the Army, were respected and highly sought after. His hazel eyes squinted as Tiffoni and Areesa approached him.

"What do I say? I'm going to kill your daughter first chance I get," Areesa whispered to the back of Tiffoni's head, "Sir, it's nice to finally meet you," is what she said instead.

"How are you," he turned his head slightly to see the white letters of her name etched upon her nameplate, "Davis?" Areesa looked at Tiffoni for more to say. Tiffoni only smiled, she knew Areesa was at a loss for words.

"How was your trip, Sir?" Areesa asked.

"I take it Tiffoni failed to tell you that her old man serves too."

"That's putting it lightly," Areesa thought smiling at him, "No Sir, I think she mentioned it. I just forgot," Areesa smiled and shrugged her shoulders hoping Tiffoni would jump in at any time.

"Areesa, yes I told you my Dad was serving this great county of ours. Remember? When we first met?" Areesa looked at her and half-smiled, thinking, "You're just full of surprises, Buddy."

For a clean-shaven hazel-eyed wheat-colored fifty something man he was attractive, Areesa thought as she, two Drill Sergeants, and Tiffoni listened to his continuous talking. Immediately following her thoughts, da-ja-vue came over her. She shook it off. She remembered when she saw him on the cover of the Army Times. A head shot of him sitting at a cherry wood desk at the

Pentagon looking straight at the camera. Even on the cover, his eyes seemed as if he was able to look through her. The article quoted him as saying, ". . . he's hard, but fair." She remembered thinking he wasn't someone she'd want to rub the wrong way. Beyond all of that, she never envisioned *him* as Tiffoni's father.

"Young lady, praises are in order. Tiffoni told me last night that the two of you both received awards. Congratulations." Areesa extended her slender hand to receive his. Her fingers easily wrapped around his large hand. As he continued to speak with Tiffoni, he held her hand in his firm grip. She felt uneasy but blew it off because she had never met anyone as well known as he was.

"Ok Dad, that's enough flirting. Let her had go, because she won't tell you to." A smile erupted across Areesa's flushed face as she withdrew her hand from his.

"Young Lady when are you going to start addressing me as Sir? You're a soldier now. It's expected. By the way your Mother sends her regrets about not being here." Tiffoni ignored his statement about her Mother while Areesa tried ignoring the Colonel flirting with her. "You two have wonderful things to look forward to. Advance Individual Training (AIT) is another great experience . . .," Areesa faded the Colonel out and focused in on the commotion across the room.

Her fellow female soldiers were freely exercising their privilege to roam about and socialize with everyone in the room, including Drill Sergeant A. Patterson. They were always talking about how good looking he was. Areesa was sure he was the talk of most letters that went home. He was the guy you'd bring home to meet Mamma and impress Daddy with. Everything about him was appealing, even when he was being mean. She could only wonder what he was like outside the barrack's site. What his laugh sounded like, what he did to kick-back. She sighed, "We don't even know his name. What am I doing? Thinking, about him, like this?" She changed her thoughts to something more constructive, like wondering what his story was: how did he end up in the army. Areesa soon found out everybody in the army had a testimony about why they enlisted.

"Thus far, he's having a brilliant career," the Colonel said snapping Areesa out of her daze. "The yellow stripes on his sleeve tell how many years he has served. From his service stripes, each representing three years, he has nine years. Let's see, from where we stand I see the Army Service and Overseas Ribbons. The Good Conduct Ribbon with one, no two oak leafs, the Army Achievement medal, ah . . . turn just a little more, Staff Sergeant . . . A. Patterson, yes a Meritorious Service and an ARCOM. The Drill Sergeant Emblem. Is he airborne . . .?" the Colonel paused briefly waiting for

Sergeant Patterson to turn a little to the left, "Of course he is. Yes, I would agree with you, he is a very impressive Drill Sergeant." Areesa was flushed and embarrassed. Tiffoni looked at the Colonel with disapproval, and he chuckled. "That's the kind of soldier you want on your team. Right Ladies?" Areesa wanted to disappear. Tiffoni shook her head side to side, her father hit Areesa's nail right on the head.

"I'll get more refreshments," the Colonel said walking away tickled by Areesa's mortified expression.

"He likes you. Don't give me that look, Areesa," Tiffoni said avoiding eye contact with her. The only person, who knows my Dad, is Drill Sergeant West. And that's because, he looked in my file, saw the name, asked me if my Dad was *the* Colonel Stryker he worked with a few years ago. I said yes and it was left at that. Believe me, he knew I didn't want to talk about my Dad or let anyone know who my Dad, the-soon-to-be General at the Pentagon, is."

"Now that I think about it you haven't said much about who you are outside of this place."

"What do you want to know? My Mom is the person I'd least want to be like. My brother is an officer serving in Italy. He's the guy who writes me all the letters. I'm a college grad with a business degree. And my Dad. What would you have me say? He speaks for himself. Though, unlike my mother, I don't ride on his coat-tail of success."

"So why not enlist as an officer candidate? I know your Dad had to trip when you said you were enlisting as a private." Areesa asked confused by her decision.

"Look at my Dad, Areesa. What do you see?" Tiffoni nodded her head up and down agreeing with impressiveness. "Yes. A Golden Boy. The crème a la de crème of the Army, and he's black. Everybody wants a part of him. You have no idea. It's endless. Some of the things I've seen and been taught to know, do, and accept for the privilege of being my father's daughter. Yea, look at him. The charming, Colonel, the confident head of the Stryker Clan, and a lousy example for fathers. My problem has always been, never accepting the place designated for me," she said sadly, "all I wanted was to see and spend time with him. The man who gave little of himself at a time in my life that being Daddy's little girl meant everything."

"I'm a Daddy's Girl and Momma's baby," Areesa said.

"I couldn't tell," Tiffoni said sarcastically. Areesa smiled proudly. Tiffoni looked down, never raising her head to look at Areesa, then she said, "I watched my Mother do for everyone else, except me. She pampers my brother because he always did, and still does, what is expected of a Stryker. Follow my Dad's lead, even if it means self-denial. I just hope my brother is a better father. As for me, it was always sit-up straight, don't do this, don't do that, you represent the family. Talk, walk, look . . . right, people will judge our family by what you do, but no room to be me. Tiffoni. Who on occasion wanted to slouch or say what really needed to be said. Money makes you phony if you don't know who you are. I know who I am, just a home-girl waiting for the ripe old' age of twenty-one."

"What's so special about twenty-one? I am past that, and I'm here to tell you, life hasn't gotten any easier," Areesa informed her.

"My family has money."

"Really, I didn't know," Areesa said mockingly.

"No Darlin', old money. My Grandparents were born and raised on the Islands, began an international investment and finance company, known today all over the world. My paternal great grandparents left the company to their oldest son, my grandfather, of whom along side my grandmother turned it in to what it is today," Areesa nodded her head understanding her family had a lot of money.

"Before my Dad and his younger brother reached child producing age, a half million dollar trust fund was established for the first born grandchild."

"So your brother gets the money. Why do the boys always get the money?"

"No. My grandmother had good sense. She wasn't having it. The original Trust is for the first-born grandchild. And you're looking at her. When I turn twenty-one, I'll have two years left before my enlistment is done. Which will help me keep my feet on the ground until I decide what I really want to do, because this," she said waving her hand around and grabbing the tips of her collar, 'ain't it."

"Let me see if I understand this. You came into the Army to irk your Mom, and sort of, in a round about way prove," Areesa said looking at Tiffoni for a confirmation as Tiffoni nodded her head up and down, "to your Dad that you can do the Army thing. Yet, embarrass him a little." Areesa continued as she put-up both her hands, displaying two fingers on her left hand, and one on the other, "Until you turn twenty-one. At which time you'll receive a now million plus Trust Fund set-up by your intelligent Grandmother, God rest her soul, who had the good sense to not limit this to the males of the Clan. Tiffoni you are rich," Areesa said in one breath.

"I know," she said leaning closer to Areesa smiling about her great plan to get from under her parents and embarrass them at the same time.

"But you act so . . . so,"

"Silly, childish. And snobbish, spoiled . . ."

"Yea, keep going," Areesa smiled agreeing with every word she said.

"None taken, Buddy," They both leaned into each other and giggled. "Just being me Areesa. True to myself. Real not a phony. It's important to me, that I know who I am before I get my inheritance."

"But you come from money. What difference does it make?"

"It's mine. No one will issue it out. No one will be able to say anything. I can do what I want, when I want. I can open up a pet store if I want. Hey, Areesa I could give it all away, if it pleases me."

"Give it away!"

"Don't worry, 'cause I'm not that foolish! This is my blessing and I want to . . .," she shhhed Areesa because her father was approaching.

"What are you two chatting about? It must be intriguing because neither of you heard nor saw me calling for Tiffoni. So what's so entertaining?"

"Father, what does Mother say about Ladies' conversation? It should never be interrupted or interrogated. Why father, Mother would be utterly disappointed, knowing you were doing both."

"I'm sure," he said. The Colonel turned and gave out a few more waves and hand shakes, while Areesa and Tiffoni snickered, at Tiffoni's clever way of getting out of answering his question. "You know, I have to be in DC, for official business tomorrow. Your Post Commander has invited me to join him and his wife this evening. Protocol. I'm sure the two of you know how important it is. You don't mind, do you Honey?"

"No Dad, of course not. I have packing to do. I'll see you at home for the holidays."

"How can he not see her disappointment?" Areesa wondered. "My Mom and Dad could immediately tell if something was wrong with me. I can't even imagine them not planning some big celebration for me. I guess … I was lucky. At least they were always there for me," Areesa thought to herself watching Tiffoni's face as she held back her tears. Areesa's eyes swelled up too.

"It's amazing. Around the eyes, you two look so much alike," he said bending over to place a kiss on Tiffoni's cheek. "Moon Eyes, I love you," he said holding her hands. "Areesa, it has been a pleasure meeting you. Why don't you join us for the holidays, if you can. The trip is on me. Tiffoni will give you my office number. Call when you're ready to make reservations," he said as he went on with his attempt to smooth Tiffoni over, Areesa realized his weakness. It was Tiffoni. It was in his eyes. He did love her, he just didn't know how to show her.

"Good-bye," he said. Tiffoni didn't get up to walk him out. She sat quietly; looking down into the half-filled Styrofoam cup, she held in her hand. She stared into it, as she gently shook and turned it to create waves and swirls in the liquid. He turned one last time before exiting. He waved and nodded his head at Areesa, who returned a nod and smile. Then he was gone.

"So Areesa, what's your story? You were so wimpy when you first came here," she said sniffling quietly, refusing to release any tears or emotions about her Dad's departure, "You seemed so sad. Alone, but not alone."

"Well, you're partially right. My Mom and Dad were killed four weeks before I came to basic."

"I'm so sorry to hear that. You must think bad of me for feeling the way I do about my parents."

"No, but I don't understand it, because my parents were there for me, always with me in everything I did. My heart goes out to you. If they were here, my Mom would probably give your Dad a piece of her mind and take you home with us, back to Jerzie."

"I've been trying to figure you out from day one. Now I understand why you're so sad sometimes. So tell me, the night Sergeant P caught you outside after lights-out, was it your parents you were thinking about?"

"Yea."

"Don't cry. It's ok. We'll be each other's family," Tiffoni said.

"Sure Buddy."

"Always remember, if you want people to think of you as strong, you have to handle your life, or your life will handle you. It's what I always tell myself as long as I know who I am, what I am able to withstand, and where I'm going, no one else really matters. Because Areesa, me, and *you* decide our own destiny."

"Tiffoni, so much has happened in my life. If only you knew."

"I'm telling you it doesn't matter. Whatever it is, it can't last forever."

"I just need some time alone, to sort things out. You know my feelings and thoughts."

"Time is the one thing no one has a lot of. I mean look, time has even run out on us. On this place." There was a moment of silence. "Why have we waited until now to get to know each other this way?" Tiffoni asked.

"Trust," Areesa said.

"Something we both seem to be lacking." The two of them sat quietly, thinking about their own future. Tiffoni laughed.

"What's so funny?" Areesa asked looking at Tiffoni.

"The one everyone calls a clown, fast and big mouth is the daughter of a soon to be Brigadier General."

"Yea, that is funny," Areesa, agreed grinning.

"Thanks Areesa."

"For what?"

"For being my Buddy."

"You're welcome."

"I think someone is looking for you."

"Who?"

"Sergeant P. Go on. We're Buddies, and Buddies look out for each other." Areesa wondered what Tiffoni thought she knew about her and Sergeant Patterson. She smiled at Tiffoni. Areesa lightly tapped Tiffoni's head and left the graduation party.

MOMENTS LATER …

Areesa was coming down the stairs from the Bay, after retouching her make-up when she encountered Drill Sergeant West. She stepped to the left side of the stairs to make way for him and sounded off.

"Go Alpha."

"All the way PFC Davis," he responded continuing his stride up the stairs. She didn't move after he passed. "Sergeant West. I'd like to say thank you. I've learned a lot about myself, and . . . I, well. I feel proud and good inside . . . thanks," she said, still at the position of attention.

"Don't get mushy on me, Davis. You dag-gone females! always getting mushy. Go on over to the Enlisted Club and help that Detail bring over more drinks." As Areesa started her decent down the stairs, Drill Sergeant West proudly said to her, "Private First Class Davis, all the way." Areesa sensed him smiling as she leaped down the stairs to do as he said.

As she strolled proudly across the courtyard in front of the barracks, she knew her platoon was the best cycle to come through in a while. Her platoon's coming was right on time because she heard through the rumor-mill their platoon was his last. He was leaving the Drill Sergeant Trail.

LATER ON…

Areesa entered the club and followed a light shining from a back room. She crossed the dance floor in the direction of the light where she encountered a civilian man coming out of the kitchen. He held three cases of sodas in his hands. "These are the last ones. You missed out," he said smiling. "Unless you want one of these," he said jokingly.

"Oh no. You look like you got it. I'll turn off the lights."

"Have it your way," he said. She laughed as she searched around the kitchen for the light switch.

"It's next to the window, to your right," the man's voice advised her. Not startled, she looked in the direction he said, because she already knew who he was.

"Thank you," she said.

"Congratulations, you're a soldier now. How does it feel to no longer be referred to as Josephine?"

"Good. What's up with Josephine any way?"

"Come on, it's the female equivalent of Joe."

"Oh," she said walking towards the refrigerator. She opened the door, looking for something to drink.

"I'll have water."

"Are you still on duty?"

"Does it look like I'm still on duty?" She turned to face him. He was wearing black slacks, a casual sweater, black shoes, and an elegant gold chain. His hair, as always, was groomed, every wave neatly in place. His mustache was neatly trimmed on his clean-shaven sable face. The fragrance of his cologne faintly drifted in the air. Not wanting him to see her blush she turned her back to him almost immediately. Facing the open refrigerator she retrieved two bottled waters. Before turning to face him again, she gave herself some advice, "Don't smile too much. Be cool. Be calm. Now turn, he's just…just a guy." Out of habit, she cleared her throat and licked her lips before turning to face him.

"Do you always lick your lips like that?"

"It's a habit, a bad one according to my, my mom," she said handing him his water. He wrapped his hand around hers and twisted off the cap. She didn't move. Not even to take a deep breath. He took the water out of her hand. She wiped her wet hand off on the side of her dress green uniform pants.

"I notice that every time I'm with you . . . you lick your lips like that. Are you nervous?"

"How perceptive you are, Sergeant Patterson." She decided to step over the boundary of what it was usually like when they were alone. "What else have you noticed?" Shocked by her question he paused and stared directly into her eyes. He took a sip of his water as she watched his Adam's-apple move up and down. He sighed after swallowing the chilled water. "So, Fort Lewis. I hear it's really nice there. Laid back, easy going. You should fit right in," he said ignoring her boldness.

"I'm sure. I hope my three months of school go by quicker than Basic."

"Are you taking leave before you sign in for Advance Training?"

"I'm putting in for fourteen days. I can do that right?"

"You sure can," he said putting his water down, then rubbing his damp hands together. "You're authorized twenty-one. Are you going home?"

"No, I'm not. I'm going to Denver to visit someone."

"Isn't Stryker from Denver?"

"Yea, but this has nothing to do with her. I'm going to see the lady who left the phone message." Wanting to change the subject she asked, "Did you know her Dad was *the* Colonel Stryker?"

"No," he said in disbelief. They both were silent for about a minute. She was leaning against a counter sipping on her bottled water and he sat on top of a table looking down at his water bottle, as he rubbed his right hand across his thigh. Areesa wanted to break the silence, by telling him why she was going to Denver. As she pondered how to tell him what was going on with her, he said, "I'm leaving the trail. I picked up my orders yesterday. As a matter of fact, I'm leaving the day after you, going to the Proving Ground." His words were sustained in time, leaving her feeling lost in the moment. Somehow she felt as long as he was there walking the halls, the Bay, the balcony, he would constantly be reminded of her . . . of them. It was bad enough she couldn't tell him how she felt. Her only compensation was, knowing he would be where they once were, long after she was gone. She looked at him wondering if she'd ever see or hear from him again. "What are you thinking about? Your eyes always give you away. When you're sad, happy, scared. Areesa, your eyes are too pretty to worry." He smiled. She made an effort to lighten up her facial expression. "I can tell when you're not OK, especially when you look the way you do right now. What's wrong?"

"I just wanna," she sighed," I want you to know I appreciate you looking out for me. I hope I didn't cause you too much trouble."

"Don't worry about it. It's all in the past. Remember when I told you there's a place and time for everything? Always believe in that, OK."

"OK. I will." She thought to herself, "Oh God, why does my heart ache like this when I'm around him? Why can't I say what I want to say to him?" After her private prayer she stepped out in the moment and told him, "You do make me nervous."

"Don't be. It's not my intent to make you nervous. Maybe after we get settled at our new duty stations, we can hang out together. You know go out to eat or something like that," he smiled at her, "You're very beautiful. I would consider it an honor to hang out with you."

"Thank you."

"I'm taking thirty days leave before I sign in. I'd like to look you up once I get situated. Is that cool with you?"

"I'd like that."

"Be good to yourself, Areesa. When it seems like you can't go on, remember Basic. That's one of the special things about it, knowing you made it through a lot of hard work and unknown challenges is an accomplishment within itself. That, alone should give you strength and motivation to go on. And don't forget your faith." He stood up and walked behind the counter to get a piece of paper and something to write with. "Take this. It's a number where I can be reached while I'm on leave. Use it if you need to, until you hear from me again." He put the paper in her hand, and then he gently enclosed the only link between them in both their hands. He released her hand, and cupped her face with both his hands. Hesitating, he knew it still wasn't their time. He traced her brow with his finger . . . then her nose. He wanted to kiss her, but instead he whispered into her black thick hair as his head rested against her's, "Don't tremble . . . don't be afraid, I promise I won't hurt you." She wrapped her arms around his waist. A moan escaped her partially parted lips, as she closed her eyes and inhaled his scent. She felt his arms enclosing her. She couldn't imagine herself any place else but there in that kitchen with him.

"Remember us, Areesa."

"I will," she said holding onto him, as tight as she could.

"Davis," a female voice yelled out from the other side of the kitchen. Sergeant Patterson easily, took a few steps away from her. "If you need me, call. Ok. Take care, Areesa," he said, feeling sad about saying good-bye, because he didn't expect anyone like her to come into his life. Silently they looked at each other, then she called out, "I'm coming," as she walked passed him towards the door. She didn't look back. He turned only catching a glance of her leaving. He walked towards the back door, and turned off the light before leaving.

see ya, Buddy

"Good Morning Alpha Company," Tiffoni yelled as she sat on her bed stretching her body. "This is a grand day, ladies. Get up and be in it."

"It's 4 a.m.. Somebody shut her up."

"Davis, get your Buddy."

Tiffoni got out of be and eagerly left Alpha Bay, headed towards the other end of the hall to make sure Gill and Yates had done her and Areesa's uniforms and to give them their list of details.

"Tiffoni, did you go down there messing with those girls?" Areesa asked, rolling out of her bunk.

"Areesa. Of course I did. And Gill wanted to get an attitude."

"Well, Tiffoni . . ." Areesa began, but Tiffoni cut her off.

"When are you going to tell me what happened last night with Sergeant P?" Tiffoni whispered. Areesa reached under her pillow and took out the paper he gave her with his number on it and stared at it. "Did you know this is his last cycle too?" Areesa asked.

"No."

"It is."

"So, what's up? Are you two going to keep in touch?" she asked leaning over to see what was written on the paper.

"I don't know. I have to take care of some things first."

"Like what? Is it something to do with your parents?"

"Yea. Tiffoni if you found out that something wasn't as it appeared, would you want to find out what happened or just leave it alone?"

"It depends on what it is. If it was life threatening I'd try to find out. Is your situation life threatening?"

"Sort of. Yea it is. Nothing I thought was the truth is. My parents, well one of my parents . . ."

"Here's your junk." Gill said dropping their shoes and clothes down on Areesa's bunk.

"Gill. You're a bad loser. But, I'm not going there with you. You see Private Gill, I don't have a problem telling your Drill Sergeant about your bad attitude. Now pick it up." Gill picked the things up off Areesa's bunk. "Where do you want this stuff?" she asked. Without looking at her Tiffoni pointed to Areesa's locker. Areesa dropped her head on her pillow, amazed by Tiffoni's heartless temperament that would creep up without warning.

It bothered her to have someone waiting on her like that, but Tiffoni on the other hand, didn't seem to have a problem with it. Areesa wondered how much money they did have, because Tiffoni seemed right at home bossing people around. Areesa, for the first time, saw something in Tiffoni she didn't like.

"Gill, it's fine. I'll do my own things. Just turn in my linen and lock, then we'll be straight."

"You're all right Davis, but your Girl be tripping. Hard." Gill looked Tiffoni up and down and walked off.

"Gill, you're going to need Yates to get all of my things downstairs to the bus. Don't be late," Tiffoni yelled at Gill's back as she left the Bay. Areesa was taking the bet all in fun, but Tiffoni was serious about them holding up their end. Areesa felt bad for Gill.

"What were you saying Areesa?"

"Nothing," Areesa said, not trusting Tiffoni, she decided to keep what Addie said about her father not being her father to herself, nor was she going to tell her she was taking her leave in Denver.

"Well, I've decided to go to Chicago, for a week and then spend a few days in Denver with my parents. Areesa are you coming to Denver? My father was serious about his invitation, you know?"

"I don't know. I might embarrass you . . . acting like common folk and all. You know Tiffoni, I've never known folks with as much money as your family . . . I'm still tripping about you enlisting into the Army. I know there's another reason for you being here. You just don't know it . . ."

"Doing my part as I wait for the world to change? Are you implying I'm meeting my destiny, Areesa?"

"Well, yea. Whose to say it's not meant for you to be here and . . ."

"And what? What other reason could there be? Stop fantasizing about the woulda, shoulda, couldas of life. It's driving me nuts," Tiffoni said leaving Areesa, sitting on her bed feeling talked down to. After a few moments of after shock, Areesa got up, walked to the back of the Bay, and saw Tiffoni sitting on an empty bunk. Her eyes looked glazed and watery. Areesa cleared her throat to get her attention "Areesa, I'm not as bad as I seem," she said staring at the eggshell wall as if it were a mirror reflecting her image back at her.

"Forget about it," she said extending her hand out to Tiffoni. Tiffoni took her hand and gave her a bear hug. "Come on Buddy lets get dressed so we can get out of here," Areesa said.

They all congregated downstairs and said their good-byes and well wishes. Areesa looked up at the window that Drill Sergeant A. Patterson, yelled at her from on her first day, telling her to double time after he nearly knocked her off her feet. She smiled at the memory. It seemed like it happened yesterday and not eight weeks ago. She wondered if he was in the building or gone already. A man appeared in the window. It was Drill Sergeant West. Areesa waved. "Do you think you'll see him again Areesa?" Tiffoni murmured quietly in her ear. Startled by her closeness, Areesa pondered her question as she stood there wanting to see him one more time. But no one came.

"I'd like to. You know Tiffoni . . .," she paused, "nothing has happened between us. He just gave me his number. How often do brothers do that? Besides, I don't even know his name." Tiffoni gave her a scrutinizing stare. "No, really. All I know is what you know, Drill Sergeant A. Patterson." Tiffoni patted her on her shoulder, in a yea-right, kinda way, and turned to get on the bus that would carry them away from the place they had come to know as home.

No more PT at 0-5-30, or eating breakfast by 0-6-still-dark-30. Or having someone in your face, telling you how to stand, walk, look, feel, or think. No more getting filthy from laying down in the mud shooting a weapon, or marching until your legs felt like cement blocks, or double timing to every place you went. No more sneaking out at night to smoke cigarettes or hanging out in the latrine putting on make-up, or mail call, or laughing and mocking the Drill Sergeants. No more talking about the future with people so different from you, that their interest in you made you feel encouraged. No more looking out for each other, or picking up the slack for the weak, and encouraging the strong to be stronger. No more unconditional Esprit de Corps, simple camaraderie. Alpha 1-5, once a family of many was now a room filled with silence. "All the way, Alpha," Areesa said softly as the words floated away into the crisp morning air.

As she looked out the rear window of the charter bus, the barracks, her home, became smaller as the miles grew wider. Sergeant A. Patterson lingered in her mind. All of a sudden, a lump formed in her throat and her heart throbbed for him. His name didn't seem so important anymore, but not knowing where he was, did.

The Bus driver chauffeured the remaining troops to their appropriate stops: Greyhound Bus Terminal, Amtrak, and the Airport, where two to five soldiers disembarked to continue the next leg of their military careers. Tiffoni got off at the Continental Airline terminal doors. "See ya. Don't forget to call about your plans to come to Denver, ok. My Family is good for the ticket, OK Areesa. Areesa promise me you'll come. Our friendship is the best thing that has ever happened to me," Tiffoni said holding Areesa's hands close to her heart. "Areesa, you've made it OK to be me. You know I was never allowed to just be me. I'm a pretender, and I'm pretty good at it, aren't I?"

Areesa smiled at her friend as her eyes filled with tears, "I'm going to miss you. Give me another hug." The two hugged and looked at each other then hugged again. The driver honked his horn. "OK, OK we're coming! Stop honking that horn," Tiffoni said wiping her tears away. "You're coming right? So I'll see ya Buddy," Tiffoni said sniffling.

"I'll let you know," Areesa said, finding it hard to say good-bye to Tiffoni. They hugged and hugged again. "Go, you're going to miss your flight and I'm going to get left," she said hugging Tiffoni once more.

"Take care Buddy," Tiffoni said waving good-bye as she entered the double automatic doors.

"Take care Buddy," Areesa said standing with her hands clasped together under her chin as she watched Tiffoni zigzag through the ropes up to the airline ticket counter. Tiffoni turned, once more, revealing her beautiful smile as she waved. Areesa smiled and waved back. The whooshing sound from the bus brakes unctioned Areesa to turn and get on the bus. Areesa paused, then turned back and watched Tiffoni as she made her way towards the terminals, as the bus doors closed. Areesa took her seat. The bus doors squealed and then slid together. The driver shift gears and the bus swayed as it pulled out of the unloading zone to proceeded to the next terminal, where she would begin her journey back twenty years into her parents' past.

She leaned back into her comfortable seat and smiled while picturing the mess Tiffoni left behind for the Drill Sergeants to find, offices trashed with pink toilet paper and red lipstick. But, not even that good happy thought could keep her completely occupied.

Ahead of her awaited answers to haunting questions that had been driving her since the night her parents died. She never did call Addie back, she just covertly planned to take her leave in Denver. Areesa felt the element of surprise would give her an edge and a sense of control. She decided to wait and call her once she was in Denver. She made her reservations after Drill Sergeant Patterson told her she could take a longer leave. Sergeant West did ask, why she was going to Denver.

Areesa felt surer of herself, since that afternoon in Ms. Mill's classroom. She knew she needed to do what Sergeant West said all female soldiers should do- "man-up". She hoped her own emotional state of being would help her face whatever her parents faced such a long time ago. As Areesa prepared to go back in time, she was beginning to experience something she hadn't truly lived yet- in spite of who people appear to be, it should never overshadow the fact that they are individual people doing the best they can as they travel through life. Her conflict with what is, and what's suppose to be was urging her to go and see this woman, Addie.

the journey home

"At this time, please buckle your seat belts and prepare for landing. American Airlines would like to thank you for flying with us and we hope to serve you again."

Areesa's seat was in the center of the plane. She closed her eyes, took a deep breath and squeezed the arms of her seat as the airplane thumped against the pavement. She relaxed when she felt all the tires touch the earth again. She patiently waited for most of the passengers to get off the plane because she knew no one was waiting for her. Tears slowly rolled from her large oval eyes, down her chestnut brown checks, making their way to her chin, finally resting in her lap. Those familiar spells of sudden sadness had not happened to her in a while. She thought she was over the stomach binding sadness that made her life feel unbearable and unreal at the same time. Knowing she was in Denver made her feel as if she was living someone else's life. The choking fear she felt after her parents died crept up inside of her soul so strong she didn't want to get off the airplane. She gripped the armrest of her chair until her veins began to protrude. An Attendant came to her, kneeled down beside her, and began rubbing the back of her hand. The two of them sat there for a minute or two, without saying a word. The attendant simply rubbed Areesa's hand. Areesa finally felt stable enough to stand. The attendant helped her gather her things. They walked to the front of the plane to the ramp leading into the terminal. Before disappearing into the tunnel, Areesa turned to look back at the attendant, wanting to say thank you, but she just waved, and continued her journey into her parents' past.

After getting her one piece of luggage, she headed for the streets of Denver, Colorado. She took a shuttle bus into the heart of the city. Denver didn't seem like a place her parents could have felt comfortable in because of the massive buildings, the close proximity of the houses, the city lights, traffic, and people moving about doing their own thing. As the shuttle bus made its way down Colfax Avenue into downtown, passing by the gold domed City Capital, into the mist of tall sleek high-rise buildings, she was finding it very difficult to imagine them there.

The city's enormous presence didn't mirror the lifestyle she and her parents lived. The life she never questioned before their deaths. Until she enlisted, she thought her life with her parents was the way everyone lived, reserved, and quiet. Areesa and her parents spent all of their time together in New Brunswick a small college township in Jersey. Their home was a modest unpretentious three-bedroom ranch style house surrounded by trees. So many trees surrounded and hovered over the cozy house that on bright sunny days Areesa could barely see the sky. She would walk across the street to sit in a field just to see the blue infinity of the sky. Often her mom expressed undecided love for the trees. Some days she spoke well of the trees' protection and on other days she felt regret about how much the trees enclosed their house. It was during her second week of Basic did the level of isolation she shared with her parents become evident, and her parents' idiosyncrasy began to seem unusual. Like the time her mom went with her into the field to look at the sky. Soon after that first walk, her mom wanted to trim the big tree near the driveway back so she could see past it from her bedroom window. She would sit for hours facing west, looking in wonderment, beyond where they lived, as if she was looking back to where she couldn't go. Then her father. He always, always walked her the two blocks to her school bus until she finished high school. And how they only went out for groceries, to pay bills, school conferences, and other necessities. Not until after their deaths did she realize how confined they were by routines, and from others. The more she thought about the way they lived, the more questions she had, about what made them live their lives the way they did.

. . . HER ARRIVAL

The hotel sat nestled in the middle of downtown. The view of the Rocky Mountains was spectacular. The snowcapped Rockies lay sprawled to the left side of the hotel. The hills and flat terrain rolled magnificently along the edge of the city as far as the eye could see.

The hotel shuttle stopped in front of the hotel and the driver helped her remove her luggage. He led her and another rider into the impressive entrance of the hotel lobby. A young guy wearing a burgundy suit jacket, white shirt with a striped black, gray and burgundy tie and black tailored slacks checked her in.

"How was your trip Ms. Davis?"

"Fine," Areesa said looking around at the different shops, boutiques, gym, pool restaurant, and lounge enclosed by glass walls.

"Your room is 222. You go down this corridor to the left where you'll see the elevators," he said giving her a card key. She entered the elevator and pressed the number two button. As she rode the elevator, she leaned on the mirrored wall, feeling exhausted, after having to get up at 4:30 a.m., thanks to Tiffoni. The nerve-racking plane ride didn't help her already over stimulated under nourished body. The elevator doors slid open and she stepped off turning right, towards her room. She walked down the corridor admiring the burgundy, green, and rosy-pink decor and beautiful pictures lining the walls anticipating her arrival to her room. She stuck her card key in the door, but it didn't work. The door beeped twice, but the card-slot red light came on. Suddenly, bouncing backwards, she realized she had attempted to open the wrong door. Looking down the hall then at the door handle, she anxiously waited for the door to swing open. Her mind said run but her legs wouldn't move. Instead, she talked to herself, "Could they be calling the front desk to report a break in? They'll know it's me. Pleeease don't nobody open that door." Her body finally got in tune with her brain, and she picked up her bags, and hurried down the corridor to find the right room. She turned the corner too fast. Her eyes broadened as she gasped for air, as a man reached out to grab her to keep her from falling backwards. All of her things fell to the floor as she flung her hands upward, attempting to block his outreaching hands. "Excuse me," the man said, holding Areesa by the upper portion of her arms, "I didn't see or hear you coming. Are you ok?" he asked. Areesa put her hands over her mouth to keep from screaming. "Yes ... I am," she stuttered, while fighting the urge to pee on herself, and the pretty carpet. "Oh, yea sure, I'm fine," she said. "I'm ok," she repeated pulling her arms away from him.

"I hope I didn't scare you," he said.

"No. No, you didn't. I should watch where I'm goin'." The man asked her again if she was ok, then he hurried off to catch the elevator. Shaking her head side to side, she let her body rest against the wall. "You've got to get a grip on yourself, and for goodness sake, stop bumping into men like this!" she said lifting her body off the wall. She made her way down the corridor to the *right* room. Once inside her room she dropped her bags on the floor and fell on the queen size bed laughing hysterically. She sat up wiping the tears from her eyes, thinking she would never tell anyone about this, except Tiffoni of course.

Areesa began unpacking, still giggling about what happened. If Tiffoni was with her, they'd still be sprawled out on the floor laughing. As she unpacked, she set aside things for a bath. A warm bath, a luxury she had not indulged in for eight weeks because in the barrack's latrine there were no bathtubs. She stayed in the tub for about twenty minutes soaking her body, taking in deep breaths of the lavender fragranced bath crystals. She had to sneak and buy the spa bath gift set, and then hide it in her personal drawer during basic if she didn't want it taken away because it was considered contraband. She got out of the warm water and laid across the beautifully made bed, she didn't pull the covers down, because she felt warm and cuddly wrapped inside her tan and white terry cloth robe. She drifted off into a restful sleep.

Areesa was awaken by the sunrise dawning through the room's large open window and an uncomfortable achy stinging feeling afflicted her hands. She shook her hands frantically attempting to loosen up the stiffness and get her blood circulating again. After gaining some feeling, she reached for the phone sitting on her night table, but the cord wouldn't extend far enough to rest on her bed. She stood up, and began pulling at her robe that was twisted around her body. Tugging at the belt, she freed herself from the tangled mess, then she realized she had overslept by an hour. She rushed to the desk to get her address book. She thumbed through it, found Addie's telephone number and dialed it.

"Hello."

"Hello, Ms. Meaks, this is Areesa."

"Areesa, I've been so worried about you. Are you just receiving my message?"

"No. I'm here . . . here in Denver. I'd like to stop by and see you today."

"Why, yes. That's a good thing. I'll be waiting. I'm eager to see the young woman you've become. Is there anything special I should have waiting for you?"

"No. That won't be necessary," she said followed by a few moments of silence.

"Are you still there Ms. Meaks?"

"Yes," Addie said.

"I'll see you soon," Areesa said. She replaced the receiver down, without saying good-bye or waiting for any more questions. A sudden breeze entered the room giving her a chill. Sill feeling susceptible to the draining feeling lingering in her body and mind, she decided to indulge, once again, in a relaxing bath instead of lying back down.

She stepped into the tube filled with tepid steamy water. Her knees popped up in the center of the water. She grabbed her bath towel and laid it across her knees to keep them wet and warm. She closed her eyes and let the warm water soothed her, as she reflected back on her last night with Sergeant A. Patterson. She took deep breaths, and remembered the smell of his cologne and the starch in his BDU uniform, "Mmm . . .," she hummed. She thought about him all the time. She liked thinking of him, how he was a *man's man*, how special she felt when she was with him. The specialness she felt was a different kind than what she shared with her parents or Ms. Mills. She felt like a woman, *the* woman good enough to capture his attention, and she felt passionate every time she was near him. "And I don't even know your name," she thought.

... LATER IN THE DAY

Denver's street noise was foreign but exhilarating to Areesa as she stood in the crisp night air waiting for a cab called for her by the hotel Guest Specialist. After about five minutes, a cab pulled up and she jumped in. She rubbed her hands rapidly together, to warm herself. She memorized the directions and advice Addie had given her about being cautious with the drivers. "Make them think you know where you're going, or they'll take advantage of you," was the best advice she had given as far as Areesa was concerned. Areesa felt it ironic, Addie would lookout for her in a motherly way, after her confession about her Dad.

Areesa believed Addie knew exactly why her parents chose not to tell her the truth before their deaths. The question was, how much was Addie going to tell her? The driver took her exactly the way Addie said he should. She exited the yellow cap and then paid him, looking him in his eyes saying, "Thank you," with an underline meaning- for not taking advantage of her.

"Very nice," Areesa said, giving Addie's house and neighborhood a good looking over. Addie lived in a three-car garage, two story bricked country estate. The beautiful house lightened Areesa's heart a little. She was actually expecting Addie to live in a rundown neighborhood, in an old beat up building on the fourth floor, with a broken elevator. Her mind was prepared for when she would have to climb the flights of stairs. She knew every stair she would have to walk up to confront Addie would flame her anger. "Well there goes that image," she thought, standing under an arched front porch foyer held up by white pillars. She could see the second floor of the house from where she stood on the porch. The lights from inside the house illuminated a beige radiant glow through the large bay glass windows on the left and right sides of the front door entrance. Areesa could see a beautiful chandelier above the front door through an elegant glass window. The lighting was just enough to let someone see the foyer and circular staircase leading to the second floor landing. Areesa's heart was thumping, firmly against her chest. She pulled her coat away from her body, shaking it to calm herself. She pressed the doorbell and glanced around the outside grounds of the house, keeping her feet in place while twisting her body around, snooping to get a first glimpse at the mad-evil woman who was trying to destroy what was left of her parents' lives. As she waited, she stood on the tips of her toes wanting to see her coming, hunched over, dragging her left foot, struggling to get to the door. No one was coming. Feeling impatient and a little testy, she rang the bell again. "Come on. Come on," she said reaching out to ring the bell again, but the door leisurely opened and a small, honey-brown woman stood before her, wearing a black uniform. Areesa drew her head back, looking the small framed woman up and down. She invited Areesa in. "Oh, a maid?" Areesa whispered.

"May I ask who's calling?"

"Ugh, A . . . A, Areesa," she stuttered.

"Ms. Meaks is expecting you. Please come in." Areesa stepped in onto a beautiful polished burnt orange wooden floor. The woman held her hand out towards her. Areesa looked around the room, then at her extended hand, not realizing what the she was waiting for. "Oh yea, sure. My coat. Here you go," she said taking her things off placing them into the woman's hands. "Oh, you're very kind, but this isn't necessary. I can hold on to my things," she said feeling somewhat uncomfortable. "Tiffoni's house probably has someone to take your gloves, another for the coat, and somebody else for your hat," she thought as she politely smiled at the woman. The woman returned a smile.

"Ms. Meaks is waiting for you in the sitting room." Areesa followed her down a hall. As she walked behind her, she peeked in every direction checking out the beautiful furnishings and decor. The closer she came to finally meeting Addie, the more she got her mind off the beautiful house, and focused on what she was there for. She began envisioning her responses syllable by syllable. As Addie drew near, Areesa fine-tuned her counter attacks against her. As she followed the maid she mumbled softly what she was going to say. They stopped at varnished French doors. The woman grabbed the two brass handles and opened the doors. Areesa hesitated before she stepped into the most beautiful room she had ever seen.

Hues of soft crimson peach and mother-of-pearls adorned the spacious room. Arrays of different textured peach and beige pillows were thrown about two large over stuffed sofas. Though the room had a comfortable inviting atmosphere with a subtle scent of melon, soft lighting, alluring colors, Areesa willed herself to stay on guard as she anticipated coming face to face with the big boned bronze woman sitting comfortably on the sofa facing the large arched windows. Areesa stepped into the room. Her feet sank into the lush beige carpet as she approached Addie sitting, untroubled, sipping a warm beverage.

Addie was not who Areesa anticipated. She was a real person. Not some wicked feeble-minded person wanting and waiting to devour what was left of her life. Instead of feeling empowerment, she felt fear in her heart. Addie stood and extended her hand. Areesa stepped back. She reminded herself she wasn't there to make friends, she only wanted answers. Addie acted as if she didn't mind Areesa's reaction. "My, my, my, Ginny's baby girl," she said retaking her seat on the sofa. She gestured for Areesa to take a seat. Areesa quietly looked around the room, ignoring Addie's comment, when her eyes came to rest on a portrait of a young man above the fireplace mantle. "He was a very handsome man back then. Was he as handsome twenty-two years later?" Areesa hesitated, she couldn't believe what she was seeing, it was her Dad. Addie continued the one-sided conversation as she poured tea for Areesa. "I haven't seen or heard from him in twenty-two years. Did you know that?" Addie waited for a response, but Areesa didn't react. She was only listening, for now. "Please come with me Areesa. There are some things I'd like to share with you." Areesa followed her out of the room back down the hall towards a closed door that Areesa thought was probably a closet. Addie opened the door and recess lights in the ceiling automatically came on casting a soft radiance onto everything in the room. Every wall was filled with books on cherrywood shelves from the top of the ceiling to the floor. Addie entered the room, then paused when she noticed Areesa still standing in the hall. She took a deep breath, then turned and gestured to Areesa to have a seat in a hunter green chaise longue. Areesa did as she suggested. Addie leaned over her to turn on a lamp and Areesa repositioned her hands and head so that she didn't touch Addie. Sensing her uneasiness Addie said, "Look, I only want to make you feel welcomed in my home, Areesa. I'm not your enemy. I mean you no harm. Please don't make this into some . . . some kind of war of wills," she said. Areesa remained obstinate because this mood made her feel like she had *some* control. "Never, let anyone tell you, you're not Virginia Nobles' daughter," Addie laughed out loud, taking her glasses from the table drawer.

"Who is Virginia Nobles?" she asked, without thought to what Addie would say next. Addie paused. "Areesa Davis right?"

"You got it. Finally you've said something right," Areesa snidely remarked.

"No, I will not let you turn this into some kind of vindictive retribution. You know nothing about what's going on. I truly want to help you, not hurt you. From the moment you stepped through my door, you've been waiting for the chance to pounce, jump down my throat. Now, we can talk, or you can go on with this, obtuse animosity. Which would you prefer?" Addie challenged her.

"Ok you've had your say, now here's where I'm coming from. I'm here because as my mother was dying, the only name she kept repeating was yours. She said you had something to say that I needed to know. Over the past four months, my *life* has been shaken down, turned around and gutted from what I used to call my *life*. Do you know what it feels like to live with uncertainties? It feels as if someone has punched me in the stomach for no reason." Addie tried to respond to her question but she was cut off by Areesa's forceful tone. "No. I'm not finished. It's an awful feeling. I feel abandoned, confused, sad all the time, and I don't understand why. My parents' dying was an accident. No one could have predicted a car accident would take them away from me, that's tangible, a reasonable explanation for how I often feel. But there is no way I could have known that not only would I have to deal with their deaths, but I was going to have to deal with secrets that they purposely kept from me. That's not tangible, explainable. I am so dag-on tired of feeling the way I do, a state of what-is-this," she expressed through clinched teeth trying not to be overtaken by her pain, "my parents have done, kept from me. No this is not reasonable to me because I don't understand what is going on. It's in conflict with every part of me that is trying to get back to a life without them. So, understand this. I have enough friends. I don't need anymore. I've had it up to here," she flung her right hand through the air, "with concerned people. I don't need them anymore," her voice trembled with rage as she went on, "The people that I thought truly loved me, are dead. There's only one thing I need now, and that's answers to my questions, and you're the only one who has them. So please, please save your friendship and concern, and just give me what I came here for! Answers about what happened to my parents when they lived here," she said as tears rolled down her face. Addie sat stun and motionless. After a few moments of silence, she lifted herself up from the chair and forced her feet to move towards another book on the shelf. As she retrieved the book she longed for the warm feeling she always felt whenever she was in her library. She gently, lovingly, removed an old leather tinseled bible with rusted bullion angles on each corner, and barely visible embossed red lettering on the front cover. She went to another shelf and removed a worn black clothed photo album that once had white pages that were now golden yellow. Wounded by Areesa's declaration she steadied herself before turning to face her again. She finally turned and walked back to her chair. She placed the books on the center table, in front of Areesa. Then she laid out the past before them both.

Addie's heart was filled with sorrow, as she accepted her lost chance to unite with the only hope of goodness from a horrible past. She mourned inside for the gone expectation of making the past right. The only thing she could give Charlie and Ginny, *truth, honor*, was being ripped from her by the person who could give all of them forgiveness. "You may never understand this. I can only pray that you find forgiveness in your heart for all of us. Especially Charlie and Virginia … they loved you so." Areesa was unmoved by her sympathetic words. Addie continued, "I knew your parents very well. Virginia," Addie said, then looked into Areesa's face, hoping not to see contempt, but she did. She cleared her throat, and refereed to Virginia as Ginny. "Ginny was my best friend and Charlie was my brother." Areesa sat attentive and still while Addie lay bare all of their hidden past. "Ginny fell in love with one of the most popular boys in our high school. We called black folks like him a wanna-be. You see, he lived outside the poverty stricken Lower End we lived in, but back then there was only one school for black kids who were in the 6th through 12th grades. He was handsome and from a prominent family. His name was Rowan, but we called him Ro. Ginny unexpectedly became pregnant by him. For Ginny, having a baby for the man she . . . well, thought would want to be a father was the best thing she could have ever hoped for. Life was hard for her, for all of us back then. Our moms were trying to make it, survive the poor housing and bleak futures ahead of all of us. Secretly I think we all wanted what the *wanna-bes* had. Well, that is everybody except Charlie. Principled Charlie. For all of his warnings …. Ginny got pregnant. After she told Rowan she was pregnant . . . well, he wasn't very happy about that bit of news. He told her to have an abortion, and Ginny refused. He put fear in her, telling her she'd be on her own if she went through with the pregnancy. If she tried to get money from him or his family, he'd destroy her, even threatened to kill her if she told anybody he was the father. She was devastated, and very afraid of this side of him that she had never seen, nor expected. You know affluence can do that to a man, give him a false right to impose retribution on anyone who does not go along with what he wants. Back then the idea of him wanting to be with her, did make her feel special. It hurt her, a great deal to know she was only good enough to sleep around with. Funny though, how she was not allowed in his world, but his false sense of privilege pride often brought him down where the poor black folks were living. Your mom, Virginia Noble," she affectionately said her name, "was our neighborhood symbol of the future. Beautiful, intelligent, ambitious, out spoken and going somewhere with her life, we both were. But she was much bolder than me," Addie humbly confessed. "We all liked seeing her with him. Living vicariously through them nurtured our own futures. Anyone who saw them walking through the neighborhood knew she belonged in his world, not ours. They'd stroll down the street holding hands, smiling, looking perfect together. After she told him she was pregnant, he told her she'd never be good enough to meet his people. That's when she knew she couldn't ignore his threats." Addie looked into Areesa's heartbroken brown eyes that reminded her so much of Ginny. They were glassy, but no tears fell. That's the way Ginny looked when she sat on Addie's bed and told her about Rowan's reaction about her being pregnant. Addie went on. "So, Charlie," Addie smiled and sighed, "sweet Charlie. He adored your Mom. From the first time he first meet her, just as we were all entering our junior year in high school. You see Charlie lived in New York, with out grandparents, for a while because our mother was having a difficult time controlling him and his zealous temperament and contempt for the conditions blacks endured here in Denver. One day when she came home with me to work on a school paper, I could see him falling in love with her. During her pregnancy, they became great friends. Oh, I suppose . . . for Charlie it was love, but for your Mom, it was safe. Comfortable. Don't get me wrong, she deeply cared for Charlie, but I don't think she loved him, not like he loved her, not back then. Well, for some reason, your real father, Rowan decided he wanted you. Without any warning, he just showed up with a changed mind, but not a changed heart. He did a hundred and eighty degree turn. All of us knew, something wasn't right. We just didn't know why he wanted to take you from your mother once you were born. I guess he wanted a namesake, we all assumed. You know back then having a child to carry on your name was important, but Ginny . . . oh, she wasn't having it. Quiet Ginny, the calm peacemaker of the neighborhood, cursed him so bad . . . oh, I tell you, she was irate." Addie shivered at the thought of him bringing out such an ugly side of her. Then you were born, your Momma was so happy. She always referred to you as a rising star. So she named you Ariisa." Tears were flowing freely, down Areesa's face, as she sat silently absorbing every word Addie said. Addie wanted to reach out and take her in her arms, but she knew Areesa wouldn't allow it. "Rowan waited until she brought you home, February second . . . before he made his attempt to take you from her. We were in disbelief! I mean, he honestly thought she was going to turn you right over. Well, Charlie was infuriated by Rowan's sudden display of fatherly interest. He knew Rowan was up to no good. From the time Charlie came back here to live, those two hated each other. Whenever Rowan would come to our neighborhood, he and Charlie would bump heads. Charlie saw in him all the ugly things money brought out of a person. Well, Charlie confronted him." Areesa's lips slightly parted to absorb a breath of air, anticipating the painful outcome. "And they struggled." Areesa released her breath. "Charlie never told me exactly what happened during their struggle. He did say something about hitting Rowan, but he was still alive when he dumped his body in an ally. Ginny waited for Charlie at the apartment. The plan was to confront Rowan. To find out what he really wanted. If they couldn't figure it out, you, your Mom and Charlie, would leave Denver, and start a new life. I was supposed to keep them informed about what was going on back here. And as soon as they knew it was safe, you all would come back home. When Charlie got back to his apartment he called an ambulance, but they got to Rowan too late. He was dead."

"My God. What have yous done!" Areesa softly asked, in disbelief.

"No Areesa, hear everything. Rowan, was shot by someone else. By the time I heard this, you, Ginny and Charlie were gone," Addie painfully shouted out, "I tried everything within me to find all of you. But It was hopeless. Now I know why. When you all left it was Charles Meaks, Virginia Nobles . . . and Ariisa, A-R-I-I-S-A, not Areesa or Ginny. I was the only person who called him Charlie, not even your Mom called him by that name. New names, new everything. Charlie made me promise . . . oh, he made me promise, he said never look for us, were my brother's last words to me," she said slumping back into her chair like she did, twenty-two years ago, "So when you called I knew. I knew they were both dead," Addie said overcome with sorrow.

Addie's revelation was the penetrating force that shattered the shield she had encased her heart in. She felt her body sinking into the chair. Willingly Areesa submitted herself to the devouring pain, simmering in her soul since her parents' deaths. Disappointed beyond what she thought she was capable of feeling, she felt as if she was plummeting into hopelessness. Lifting her palms up towards her face to wipe away tears, "My life ... I just don't understand, and no matter what I do this madness just won't stop! Why Mommy, why? What am I suppose to do ... it just keeps coming, and coming. You and Daddy, your lives aren't lining up, with what's happening ... I don't understand, why. You know what, I can't stop thinking ... living they protected me, dead they're destroying me. I went to *them* for help during moments like this, for advice ... protection . . . who do I go to now to protect me from them," she cried.

Her once precious memories of the two people who loved her endlessly, laid bare before her as two people who were on the run for murder. The murder of her real father. Her parent's lives unraveled before as deceptive, suspicious. She didn't know what was true about them anymore as her memories of them began falling down all around her making her life seem more and more unreal. The constant moving during her early childhood. It wasn't until her eight-grade year did they finally settle in the house they left to her. No friends slept over at her house, nor did she sleep at someone else's house. Her Mom sitting for hours staring out of a bedroom window and they would go to the store separately. She remember asking why they all never went into a store together, and they told her if something happened to either of them who would be there to take care of her. It sounded so reasonable to her back then. It was only during her first year in college did her parents travel long distance without her. All of the long talks about respect and doing right by others. How many times she was told to talk things out and that people are generally good. "Lies, lies, lies. It was all a lie," she said shaking her head side to side. Areesa stood up and attempted to compose herself, but she couldn't, because of the shaking rage welling up inside of her. She looked at Addie, then turned, and ran out of her house. Areesa did what she knew she did well, she ran leaving her coat and who she was before she entered Addie's house behind. Addie ran after her. "Areesa. Areesa, please, don't go. Wait! Let me help you!" Areesa's ability to run took over like it always did when she didn't want to deal with what was before her. She leaped off Addie's front porch onto the lawn and ran through her flowerbeds, across the manicured lawn onto the street in the direction she came. Addie tried to catch her, but it was useless. "Areesa, Areesa, we loved you. We only wanted to protect you. Areesa! Areesa, please forgive us! Please forgive us," Addie shouted as she watched her disappear into the darkness.

Unmoved by Addie's cries to come back, Areesa kept running. Faster and faster, she just wanted to run, keep running, until she was as far away as she could get. Not knowing where she was, she ran towards the city's illuminating glow above the trees. She felt the cold rushing air and misty rain against her face and bare arms, but her shivering didn't stop her from running. She didn't care, she just kept running, away from her dishonor; thinking she was going to set Addie straight! Get her told off for telling lies about her parents. Now that she knew the truth, what she wanted more than anything was to get back to her hotel room, pack her things, and leave Denver.

Still running, she emerged out of a neighborhood into the streets of the city. She ran through a park and exited on Colfax Avenue. She tried getting across the busy street to the cluster of tall buildings that where no longer distinctive to her eyes. She couldn't figure out which way to go to get back to her hotel. She stopped running and walked quickly pass a Cathedral that sat almost on the curve of the street. Still unsure of where she was and unable to recognize the hotel she was staying in, she stepped onto the streets into the pathway of cars. Drivers honked their horns and screamed at her.

"Get out of the street you nut!"

"What's your problem lady?"

"Yo, get out of the street," someone else yelled. Areesa could hear what they were saying, but she couldn't see any of their faces because of the headlights shining her face. She was spinning, holding her head and ears, praying that everyone would go away and leave her alone. She managed to cross the street, still looking around for something familiar. While people began gathering around her, she pressed her way through the crowd, running towards something familiar, a payphone. She grabbed the receiver. Shaken, cold, and scared she dialed the operator and ask to make a collect call. She gave the operator the number without thinking.

"Hello," a man's voice echoed through the receiver.

"Sergeant Patterson?" she cried into the voice piece.

"Hold on," Sergeant West said. He knew who she was. Sergeant West pushed the hook on his phone twice. He said to the man's voice that answered,

"Hey man, it's her and she's crying," he calmly said as he laid his receiver down on the kitchen counter and walked away.

"Areesa? Areesa where are you?" Sergeant Patterson asked.

"Please, help me . . . I-I'm lost," she cried into the telephone, "Help me, I don't know where else to go. There's no one else for me to call. Please, please tell me what to do."

"Where are you? Tell me where you're at."

"I don't know where I am!" she said. He knew he had to calm her down if he was going to help her through this.

"Areesa, please . . . you have to tell me where you are. I can't help if I don't know where you are. Please Areesa, you have to try."

"I went to see Addie . . ."

"I don't care about that. Just give me the name of a street, or a building. Anything. Baby, you've got to help me find you," he pleaded with her. She didn't respond. "Areesa, Areesa, don't go Areesa," his voiced traveled through the phone into the air. Areesa was gone.

Sergeant Patterson hung up the phone, grabbed his jacket and keys and ran out of the room into the streets of Denver. Areesa had no idea where he was. She didn't know the number he had given her was Sergeant West's home number. Sergeant Patterson pre-planned with his friend, to receive her call just in case she needed him. Based on what he found out about her past during Basic, he knew something was about to confront her that she couldn't handle alone. No one could.

He drove through the streets, slowly turning corners, stopping at allies, looking into people's faces as he passed them by, trying to find her. "Hang in there Baby, I'll find you." As soon as the words left his mouth, he saw her. He turned his car onto the next one-way street to circle around behind her. Without warning to any of the other drivers, he began dodging through traffic, trying to get to her. He blew his horn while shouting "Move," to every person who got in his way as he drove forward weaving in and out and around cars until he was unable to drive the car any further. He pulled his car close to the curve, jumped out and ran down the street onto the sidewalk, pushing and shoving, people from his path as he made his way to her. "Areesa wait," he shouted. She stopped and turned at the calling of her name. She saw him running towards her, but the misty rain and her tears made her feel unsure, unknowing as to who was calling her. Closer and closer, and closer he came, she was afraid to believe her eyes. She thought she was imagining him, like she imagined her parents out in the crowd waving and calling her name on graduation day. She wasn't sure about anything anymore. Areesa just stood still and closed her eyes, giving up to the burden that was weighing her down, she had had enough. Feeling lightheaded, her body swayed. Areesa collapsed, once again, into the arms of Staff Sergeant A. Patterson.

conflict

Areesa awaken. She quickly sat up, looking around the room for something familiar. She lifted the king size white down comforter, and she was wearing her same clothes. She just didn't know where she was. From the living room area of his hotel room Sergeant Patterson heard her moving about. He got up from his seat and walked into his suite's bedroom where she was.

"It's ok. You're in my hotel room."

"Oh."

"Are you feeling al'ight," he asked her leaning over her. He gently brushed her hair back away from her face. She pressed her face into the palm of his hand. "You are here. You're really here," she whispered into the palm of his hand as her hand pressed his hand closer to her face. "I thought I was dreaming. But, you're really here," she said sitting-up in the king size bed.

"Yep," he said affectionately as he enclosed her slender frame in his arms, "I told you I would be here for you if you needed me."

"How. When did you get to Denver?"

"Well, when we talked in the kitchen that night I was going home. Then I watched you get on the bus yesterday morning. You looked scared. So, I asked Sergeant West for his help, changed my ticket and here I am. As a matter of fact, I saw you in the airport," he teased her.

"How much do you know?"

"I know little bits and pieces. I've spoken with Addie," he paused, "I called her to let her know where you are. You know, she's really worried about you. When we last talked, I wanted to ask if I could tag along."

"Why didn't you?"

"I felt if you wanted me to come or know what was going on you would ask or say something. Anyway," he said in a matter of fact tone, "we were still in the Basic Training atmosphere. Folks would have really started tripping if they knew we were coming here together. And in reality, we didn't come together, we just . . . sort of bumped into each other. Right?"

"Did Addie tell you anything," she asked holding her head down. He lifted her head up. "You could melt an iceberg with your eyes. Don't let the floor be the only thing that gets to admire them. You have nothing to feel ashamed about. Nothing at all." Areesa sighed, feeling relieved, and comforted by his words.

"What is your name?"

"What?" he said laughing at her out-of-the-blue question.

"Your name. What is it?" she asked again, smiling. His laugh was strong and full. She liked it. "Don't laugh. I know you as Drill Sergeant Patterson, Sergeant P, or Sergeant A. Patterson. What is you name? What does the 'A' stand for?" she said pulling him at his waist as he tried to get up, still laughing.

"Al'ight, al'ight, don't grab me like that I'm ticklish ..."

"If you don't tell me I'm going to tickle you so much that . . ."

"Ok, I'll tell you Ms. Davis," he said amused by the silliness of their play. "Antonis. My name is Antonis Keith Patterson."

"Antonis," she repeated.

"Yep, that's me."

"I like it," she whispered into his chest as she snuggled in closer to him. He took her hand and gently pulled her in closer to him, as she slid her feet from under the comforter he lifted her up into his arms. They stood in the center of the room, embracing, without worry or consciousness of place, space or time. Their moment had arrived. No one, and no rules to stop them. They allowed themselves to surrender to the sensuous feeling they felt when they were together. To have traveled so far, and finally be in each other's arms was worth every effort it took to get to their moment in time.

He had never felt the way he did when he was with her, wanting to see and be with her all time. He was glad to see her rotation come to an end because he wasn't sure how much longer he could maintain his professionalism, his military bearing when he was around her.

"Areesa I am happy you're . . . we're here together. You don't know how hard it was in Basic to be near you, and not want to touch and hold you. So many Drills were out there, having affairs, planning hook-ups, meeting in secret places to get one night of play with you guys. Until you, I couldn't understand how they could go out like that. I am sorry though, about being hard on you. I had to keep some kind of wall between us or we both would have been finished, and I didn't want us to end up like that," he said holding her as close as he could get her, without squeezing her too tight. They looked into each other's eyes and kissed. His full round lips felt better than she imagined. He drew back from her and stared into her eyes and for the hundredth time, he was still captivated by her. He wanted her to see in his face that he wanted nothing from her. He just wanted to be with her.

"Thank you for being here for me Antonis," she said kissing him on the tip of his nose.

"From the first time I saw you Areesa I couldn't stop thinking about you. I use to watch you all the time. Your smile, the way you moved. You had me goin'. And ah man, to hear you laugh warmed my heart, and the way you were always reaching out to the other females. It was nice to see someone different, from the same old lot of females, coming through." Right before his eyes a very shy Areesa emerged. She shook her head no to all he had said.

"What's wrong?" he asked.

"I feel tired, like I haven't slept in days."

"Have you?" She moved her shoulders up, then down. "You've been through a lot within the past couple of days. Graduation. Traveling halfway across the States. Come on," he said pulling her by her arm, sitting her back down on the bed, then laying her down again. He tucked her in and kissed her on her cheek.

"I'm glad you're here. Thank you," she whispered.

"You've said that already. And you're welcome." He kissed her again and left the bedroom. She heard the shower go on a few minutes later. Then he yelled out to her, "Room service will bring our food in about an hour."

"Ok," she said. At first she was afraid to close her eyes. She thought she would wake up and find that the two of them together was all a dream. She listened to him moving about. She wasn't dreaming, he was there and she was safe, so she snuggled her weary body down into the comfort of his bed and fell asleep.

The knocking at the door woke her. It was room service with their dinner. She heard Antonis direct the waiter to place the food on the table. She still couldn't believe she was with him. She rolled over and looked out the large window at the city lying serenely below. Everything was good and perfect. Only her past overshadowed the sweet peace she was feeling. She began to cry. "My Dad, he must have loved me to do what he did. He sacrificed his life to protect Mommy and me. So, why did Rowan have a change of mind and who killed him? A man like that who already had money and whatever else he wanted. Why did he suddenly want me? Maybe he wanted to take care of me. Oh, Mommy why didn't you at least give him a chance? You had to have loved him. Didn't you?" she thought.

Antonis knocking at the door interrupted her thoughts. He waited for her to say come in. He peeped into the room. She smiled at him, while brushing her hair down with her hands. He bowed his head and smiled.

"I've seen you like this before."

"Yea, but not in your room." He laughed at her response.

"You're right, and you look better here in my room. Our dinner is here," he said stepping further into the room. "Uh, I hope I didn't over step my boundary, but I got a few things for you, just in case you…, well, the bag on the chair is for you."

"Thank you," she said surprised by his generosity. While she was sleeping, Antonis shopped in the hotel stores for her. Purchasing a toiletry gift bag and clothing because he didn't know what hotel she was staying in, leaving him with no way of getting her things for her. He also purchased lip-gloss, a black eyeliner and comb and brush set for her.

After he closed the door, she got out of bed and went into the spacious bathroom. Standing in front of the large mirror above his and her sinks, she looked at her self proudly, delighted about being with him. "Wow, he likes me," she said pulling the shower curtain back, then turning on the water. She pulled up the silver handle and the water burst through the nozzle. After a few moments, the bathroom was filled with steam. The shower was soothing, just what she needed. Carefully she stepped out the shower, wrapping a white terrycloth towel around her torso. Instead of creating a visible spot on the mirror, she wrote on the steamed glass- *I'm safe*.

Areesa felt normal while brushing her teeth, applying the eyeliner, mascara, and lip-gloss Antonis purchased for her. Standing in the mirror turning to the left, then to the right checking out her hair and clothes, she felt ready for dinner with him. Taking a deep breath didn't stop her heart from pounding, so she breathed in then out again, and sighed. She clasped her hands together and said, "I'm safe," as she turned and left bathroom. Walking across the bedroom, she paused again, taking a deep breath. She turned the lights off and walked towards the door. Slowly she reached out, and placed her cold clammy hand on the doorknob, but she didn't open the door, she just stared at the knob, then the door, peering at it as if she had x-ray vision. "I'm safe," she said taking another deep breath, leaning her head against the door. She took another deep breath, placing her left hand on top of her right she turned the knob slowly, and then began pulling the door open until the light from the living room shined in.

He cleared his throat, captivate by her stunning appearance in the dress he purchased for her. A sleeveless ankle length powder blue floral dress with a white sheer underlay that clung to her upper body and flowed freely below her hips.

"Wow, the food smells wonderful, what is it?" she asked without validating his broad smile.

"Grilled Steak Verde seasoned with garlic, parsley, green onions and caper sauce, and uh, baked potatoes with butter and sour cream, fresh bread, and Copperidge White Zinfandel," he said standing to his feet as she approached the table.

"It looks delicious," she said as he pulled her chair out for her. She avoided eye contact with him as he helped slide her chair to the table. They occasionally looked up at each other and commented about the meal, or Basic, rather than take a chance on conversation that could lead to Addie or her parents. They continued their meal in silence, until Antonis felt it was time to clear the air. He offered her more wine and she declined. "Addie wants you to call her when you're feeling better. It's been an entire day, you know." They looked up from their plates at the same time into each other's eyes. Areesa didn't respond. In spite of her ability to melt his heart, he held her gaze. "Areesa, the best way to deal with things is head on. I'm not going to pretend I know how you feel, but avoiding what's happening is not the answer." He paused. "You know I'm for you," he concluded. She didn't say anything, so he added, "There is some good in this, you know your father had his reasons for what he did. Keeping it real with you, if I was him, and if your mother was anything like you, I would have probably taken some of the same actions."

"What would you have done differently?"

"I would have told you what went down when I thought you were old enough to understand. I wouldn't have waited until I was dying and left the burden on someone else to explain my actions." Tears filled her eyes. What hurt the most was- he was right. "You nor Addie should feel at fault because of how your parents handled all of this."

Areesa realized for the first time that in spite of the actions her parents took, she loved them. Though her heart felt broken, she was beginning to understand her father's decision to leave the way he did, under the conditions that he did, but it was easier for her to direct her anger at everyone else, because they were dead and couldn't face her.

She pushed her chair back from the table, Antonis stood to his feet. She stared in his eyes, wishing they could have just ate dinner. She turned and went into the bedroom. After ten or so minutes, she returned to the living area with her bag, passing by the dinner table without stopping or saying good-bye, she left Antonis' hotel suite. He looked at the door as it closed behind her. She leaned against the door that he still watched from the other side. "Please, be patient with me," she said as she made her way down the corridor towards the elevator.

From outside her hotel door she could hear the phone ringing. She fumbled with her card to get it into the slot. "Come on, come on" she said waiting to see the green light flash. The door light went from red to green. She pulled the card out of the slot while simultaneously pushing the handle down. Dropping her bag and purse on the floor, she rushed to catch the phone before it stopped ringing. She thought it was Antonis, but it was Addie.

"Areesa, I just wanted to be sure you were doing well. Your friend called and said you were, but I needed to hear from you myself." Areesa didn't respond. "Areesa?"

"Yes, I'm here. Listen, I can't do this right now."

"We have to talk. There are events I think you might be interested in hearing about." Addie paused, "Please, come to dinner. Invite your friend. He's more than welcomed to come. Areesa, I want . . . I need us to work through this together."

"I'll call you back later and let you know."

"That sounds fine, Honey. If…if I'm not here, please leave a message with Anna. I'm so happy you made it back to your hotel safely," Addie tenderly conveyed. Areesa began to cry. "I hope to see you soon," Addie concluded and hung up the phone.

Areesa replaced the receiver in its cradle and sat quietly on her bed as her tears rolled down her face. Nothing she had imagined compared to the pain and emptiness she was feeling. She couldn't understand how her parents could leave her this way; no dignity, no honor. No, it wasn't ok. What were they thinking, when they drove away with her heading to nowhere.

Slowly she rose from her seated position on the edge of the bed. She turned. She was looking at her image in the mirror. She felt disconnected from the person she saw *daddy's little girl*. The image faded to a faceless one, no longer healed by her basic training experience, but wounded. Very slowly, she took a few steps, towards a black leather chair where she carefully sat her tired body. She sat still … hushed, afraid to move. Literally, every part of her body ached with pain. Memories of her dad would never be the same … he *was not her dad*. She didn't want to hear the voices of everyone who ever saw her with her mother shouting out in her head, SHE LOOKS JUST LIKE YOU, LIL' GINNY, YOU ARE YOUR MOTHER'S DAUGHTER, YOU REMIND ME OF YOUR MOTHER. Compliments that once made her feel strong and confident, now made her cringe. Answers that only the two of them could give went with them to their graves. She thought back to how it made her feel to hear her father call her his baby girl. Now she was a face without a place, she threw the wooden business card holder set at the mirror. Anger exploded out of her, impulsively she attack everything within her path. What didn't stop the force of her anger was destroyed by her anger. Finally unleashed, her outrage came. She raked her upper body cross the desktop and everything on it slammed against the floor and walls. Turning without thought, she grabbed pillows from the beds throwing them, and throwing them again. In madness, she pulled all the linen off both beds. Entangled in it she pulled and ripped at the fabric, until her body fell to the floor. Crying uncontrollably, she banged her clinched fist on the side of the dresser, and floor. Then suddenly she grabbed her luggage from the stand and began pulling everything out of it, throwing her things on top of everything else. Clothing, shoes, uniforms, the gift bag Antonis had given her, everything flew through the air landing in many directions until all the contents laid sprawled about the room. She knocked lamps to the floor and threw the bedside phone across the room into a corner, *ding* echoed out as it landed off the hook. She staggered into the bathroom. Using her hands she raked her perfumes, bath oils, tooth paste, bottled liquids, brush and comb, hair pins, everything across the double sink counter. Glass crashed against the wall and mirror, shattering and spilling liquids. She grabbed the coffee maker, cups, and hotel amenities and forcefully threw them up against the wall. All of it falling and crashing to the floor, breaking and shattering. Out of control, she pulled down the white towels from their racks, and then she yanked and yanked at the shower curtain until the twelve clamps popped off, giving in to her strength, allowing the weight and force of her body to pull herself and everything else down to the floor on top of the debris. The smell of ground coffee, lavender bath crystals, and her perfumes permeated the air. She reached out grabbing, smashing and ripping things apart. When nothing else fell into her hands, she slammed her fist against the down lid of the toilet. "Why, why, why?" she cried out at the top of her voice, not caring who heard her screaming. She cried herself into exhaustion. All she could do was curl up into a fetal position, and moan, gasp, and heave for air until her wailing subsided into quietness. She was too fatigued to get up, so she laid on the messy cold damp bathroom floor, where she fell asleep.

Bam*Bam*Bam*Bam. Areesa was awaken by the sound at her door. "Areesa, Areesa, open this door. I know you're in there . . . open this door, Areesa," Antonis demanded. "I've been calling, Areesa. Please, let me in. I read the note you left on the bed. I will be patient, like you want me to be, but when I called the number you left and it stayed busy, I started worrying about you. Please, open this door," he pleaded. He banged his fist against the door four more times. "I know you're in there. Open the door, Baby." He stopped pounding and talking. The palms of his hands rested on the dark oak door. He leaned all of his body weight onto the closed door. Still nothing. He pushed up off the door, trying to resist kicking the door. "Areesa it took everything in me not to come over her last night, but this morning when I called and the line stayed busy I knew something was wrong. I know you're in there, you wouldn't leave without saying good-bye. Come on Baby, open the door. I know you're in there. Please talk to me. Just let me see you, and then I'll go and wait for you to call. I just need to know you're ok," he said. He paused, then pressed his ear up against the door to listen for any movement or sounds. "We, I'm worried about you. I only want to help. Let me help you." Still no answer. He started pushing his body against the door out of frustration, calling out her name. The chain from the inside of the room rattled every time he pushed up against the door. Areesa slowly uncurled her stiff cramped body out of its fetal position. She placed her right hand over her chest and pressed against it to release a painful cough. The congestion rattled in her chest. Sitting up was hard for her after sleeping on the floor all night. She paused a moment before trying to stand up. Then she used the wall to brace herself as she rose to her feet. She stumbled towards the bathroom door in darkness making her way towards the direction of the banging sound. "Wait, I'm coming," she muttered.

The door opened slowly. As the rays of day light entered the room, Areesa put her left hand to her face to protect her swollen eyes from the sunlight beaming in through the corridor windows. Her sable hair was matted to her head and face by some kind of dried yellow lotion. Her beautiful dress was torn and stained with perfumes, lotions, and blood spots. Her puffy engorged red eyes were barely open, her full lips were swollen, and clotted bruises marked her face and hands. Antonis was speechless by the sight of her, bruised, weak, sickly appearance. She released the door and turned away from him. Without concern, she walked on the mess laying about the floor, as he followed behind her trying to avoid stepping on things. Without speaking, she laid down on her sheetless bed, back into a fetal position. Antonis' eyes followed the trail of mess towards the bathroom where he could see the impression of her body on top of the debris covered floor. He paused, then took a deep breath before pushing her room door close. His eyes adjusted to the room's darkness as he stood in silence, starring around the rest of the devastated room. Not knowing what to say or think he just looked at her lying on the bare mattress. In that moment he realized he wasn't sure anymore about how to help her. His eyes filled with tears. He knew the situation was hard on her, but he was unprepared for what he saw. After taking in a few deep breaths, he turned on the soft glowing hall light. It lit the room just enough not to send his eyes or hers into shock, yet enough for him to see a little more clearly. The room was in chaos. Looking around he decided to start in the bathroom. He salvaged through the rubble and recovered several towels that were mostly clean. He shook them free of debris and began the chore of restoring order. He picked up the vanilla colored shower curtain and shook it free of fragments of broken glass. Next, he used one of the towels as a broom. The glass scratched the tiled floor like nails dragging across a chalkboard as he swept all the broken glass into a pile in front of the bathroom door. The liquids had dried on the curtain so he filled the tub with tepid water to soak it while he turned his attention to cleaning the bathroom counter. Using the second towel, he saturated it with the body soap provided by the hotel. Then he used the soapy towel to clean the stain marks from the sink, and counter. He used facial tissues to clean the chrome fixtures, giving them a spit shine appearance. Antonis checked on the shower curtain, and conceded he couldn't re-hang it because the hook holes were torn, so he rolled it up and placed it on top of the shelf inside the closet. The third towel was used as a mop to remove, tiny bits of remaining glass and dried perfumes, and bubble bath stains on the floor. He was able to salvage only the things that were in plastic bottles. Even the coffee maker was broken. He drained the tub, rinsed it out, and then ran steamy water into it. As the water filled the tub, he went to clean the room where Areesa was.

Antonis started picking up her clothes. He created three piles, things to go to the laundry, clothes to be hung in the closet, and a change of clothes for her to put on after her bath. He placed a pair of soft faded denims, a white sweatshirt, a black belt, white socks still in a military roll, and her black boots on a chair. Then he took the dirty clothes and put them in a plastic hotel laundry bag, the others he folded and put away in the dresser drawers. He went back to the bathroom, and turned off the water.

The entire time, Areesa lay still without speaking or moving as he re-established her room. Occasionally she opened her eyes, catching glimpses of him, then she'd close her eyes, and listen to his footsteps. He turned on the TV, but left the volume down, and he opened the curtains a little, giving the room a little more light. After assessing his progress, Antonis picked up fallen lamps, and rightfully replaced or straightened out lampshades. He picked up the phone off the floor, returning it to the nightstand between the beds. He lifted the receiver from the cradle and then pressed the message button, without putting the receiver to his ear, because he was certain all the calls were from either him or Addie. Once the red light stopped beeping he placed the receiver in the cradle. He lifted the leather desk chair off its side and rolled it back to the desk. Then he organized the hotel stationary and menu on the desk. He looked in the mirror, then at her, except for her chest slowly rising and falling she laid motionless and he wondered what did she see, that made her crack the mirror. He removed two pillows from the top of the dresser and placed them on the foot of the bed. He gathered four more pillows, two comforters and sets of sheets from the floor, and began making up the other bed. He fluffed three pillows, and placed them at the top of the bed. He only made the bed halfway. Then he gently lifted her up off the other bed into his arms and sat her down on the chaise. He slid the matching footstool near the chair, then covered her with a tan velour blanket, tucking it snuggly around her waist and beneath her legs and feet. Antonis turned his attention to making-up the bed she was lying on. She watched him do perfect 90 degree angles at the foot of the bed, and his large hands gently fluffed and tossed the three remaining pillows, placing them in their proper places at the top of the bed. Her eyes followed his every move, and she felt relieved knowing he was being so helpful without asking her a thousand questions that she had no answers to. He dialed the hotel operator and requested that house keeping deliver fresh towels, more amenities, another Mr. Coffee, and do a laundry pick up. After that, he dialed for room service and ordered her toast, fruit, orange juice, and milk. Having done all he could for the room, he leaned over her, and lifted her up into his arms. She held on to him as tightly as she could, as he cradled her in his arms. He pulled his head away from her, so he could see her face, but she nuzzled her face into his chest. "Baby, please look at me?" he said tenderly. She hesitated at first, then did as he asked. An overwhelming feeling of sorrow filled her heart as she starred at him. Someone knocked on the door. He placed her down on the bed, and then went to the door. It was a petite olive color woman with long black wavy hair dressed in khaki slacks, and a burgundy hotel smock, holding fresh towels in her hand like a serving tray. On top of the towels were more bathroom toiletries. She attempted to step into the room, but he stepped in front of her, taking the things and thanking her for bringing them so quickly. He placed the towels on the rack, except one hand towel, which he wet with warm water, before going back to where Areesa was. He used the warm damp hand towel to clean her face and hands. He went back to freshen the hand towel, so he could clean her hair, but when he returned he found her sitting up with her feet on the floor, her body was partly hunched over, and her hands were clamped tightly between her knees, as she rocked back and forth. He paused, wanting to give her a chance to feel free to talk, if she wanted to because since he had entered the room she had not spoken any words. He gradually approached her, and didn't speak. He kneeled down in front of her, and tenderly pulled her soiled dress from beneath her and over her head. Then he wiped her hair free of the liquids that had dried in it. He lifted her hands and cleaned the dry blood away from the cuts on her palms and knuckles. In silence he carefully wrapped her back in the blanket, as he rose up he took her hands and lifted her to her feet, and lead her into the bathroom, where the tub of hot water had cooled enough for her to get in. He sat her down on the toilet seat lid and loosened her hair. He laid her toothpaste & brush, soap, bath towel, and washcloth on the counter. He knelled down in front of her. "Areesa, I . . . ," Areesa silenced him with a loving kiss and hug.

"I'm thankful you're here with me. That's all that matters, right?" she asked in a child like tone.

"Yea, that's all that matters." He stood to leave the bathroom so she could take her bath. His hand held the doorknob, but he couldn't walk out the door. She looked at the back of him waiting for him to turn and take her back into his arms.

"Areesa, be strong. Focus on the past eight weeks of your life, how hard it was, but you did it, and you made it through carrying a load. That's what really matters, not what your parents' did or didn't do, or what Addie tells you. Because I," he said turning to look into her eyes, "believe they did what they thought was right for you at the time. Right or wrong, only here and now," he said pointing at her then himself, "is what really matters." She looked up at him. "You straight?" She nodded her head up and down. "Al'ight." She nodded yes. In that, moment she knew she could trust in what he was saying, because she believed in him. "You're different, Staff Sergeant Antonis Keith Patterson," she whispered. On those words, he turned and left the bathroom.

Standing, then letting the blanket fall to the floor, she stuck one foot into the scented balmy water causing it to swirl around. The water swished as she sunk slowly down into it. Totally enwrapped in water she quietly relaxed with her eyes closed. She thought of him; the hue of his russet complexion, his statuette frame dominated by military mannerism and the depth of his round dark eyes as she inhaled the soothing lavender scent in the water. She admired his compassion hidden beneath ordered self-discipline. She had never known a man like him. The way he was in Basic Training, focused, bluntly out spoken, raw. It seemed as if no one or nothing bothered him or could bring him down. She also recognized, during her daily secret watching of him, that his colleagues had great respect for him because he was one of the *Fellas*. Though many trainees were afraid of him, he was known for being just, and a stickler for abiding by Army Regulations. When correcting them, he would say, "Check the AR (Army Regulation), you can't go wrong if it's in the reg." She never saw him compromising his privacy, or hanging around shooting the breeze with the other Drills, he did what he had to do and he was gone. She sunk deeper into to the warm silky water, smiling.

Following her bath, Areesa felt much better. Her eyes were still a little puffy, but not as red as before. She sat on the edge of the tub, enjoying her constants thoughts of him as she got dressed. Antonis' physical appearance, as handsome as he was, would make most feel insecure, but she didn't, as she thought about how gentle his large hands were on her skin and how his muscular body didn't crush or bind her. As she put on her jeans, she sighed as she thought about how free she felt when she was enclosed in his arms. Her constant smiling validated her sense of feeling lovely in a sweet kind of way whenever she thought of him. She came out of the bathroom wanting to hug him tightly, but he was gone.

She sat on the edge of the bed and brushed her hair letting it drape down her neck below her shoulders. Looking around the room admiring Antonis' hard work, she felt hopeful and more like herself. Yet, she wondered what he thought of her after seeing her exposed as emotionally bare as a human being could possibly get.

Tiffoni was certainly right about one thing, you do decide how you will live each moment of your life, or someone else will dictate how you live, and you might not like how they go about getting it done. Areesa made a conscious decision right then to find out more about her biological father, what happened to him. She recognized Antonis was right too, her parents did what they thought was right based on what they knew about life, the world around them, and that's what she had to do if she was going to live her life. The quick knocks at her door caused her to drop her brush to the floor. "Who is it?" she playfully asked.

"It's me," he said.

"I'm coming," she said thrilled that he had returned. When she opened the door, he held his position, gazing at her, how perfect and fitting she was for him. He presented her with a plush cuddly light brown rabbit. She smiled as she pictured him in the store- A bear in a china shop, his big hand gently reaching out to pick-up a fragile rabbit. He must have felt silly walking through the corridor with this little furry rabbit in his hand, she thought smiling. She walked up to him and buried her face in his chest, and giggled.

"Antonis, you're spoiling me."

"Yea, I am," he said pleased to see her smiling again. He stepped into the room after kissing her on her forehead. "Come on, lets go," he said grabbing their jackets.

"Go where," she asked giggling at his playful behavior.

"To the park."

"The park?"

"Yea, I love parks," he said pulling her out the door.

the park

Antonis left the room to lease a white SUV. Knowing he was leaving tomorrow, he wanted to see her happy, and spend time with her not overshadow by her parents. She deserved it.

They headed towards Interstate-70. As they rode through the green rolling hills and alongside snow capped peaks, Areesa put her hand out the window; she couldn't resist attempting to reach for the clouds that appeared to be at her fingertips despite the cool air against her skin. Antonis laughed at her rowdy screams. He couldn't help thinking how radiant she looked in a pair of jeans and sweat shirt. He caught her gleaming eyes and she smiled at him, and then returned to her rowdy behavior as they traveled across Colorado's scenic highways. Breathlessly her eyes wondered and marveled. She had never seen anything more beautiful than Denver's Rocky Mountains. He laughed when she would stop talking, and say, *awe* when she discovered another beautiful cotton ball cloud drifting across the never-ending mountainous landscapes & peaks, as they drove listening to music on the radio talking about everything and nothing.

As they pulled into a gas station Antonis teased her about not having her driving license, if not for the Army. He kept telling her the Army only issued cracker-jack licenses and she laughed because she had never heard that before.

Areesa enjoyed the way they laughed together, because her best fantasy about being with him did not measure up to actually being with him, and she was enjoying every second. She told him, "This makes up for you being mean to me." He laughed.

"Have you ever pumped gas before?" he asked.

"If I tell you no, then you're going to want me to do it, for the experience, and I don't think so," she responded trying not to smile at his pouting face.

"OK-OK, I promise, I won't let you pump gas, just tell me."

"I've never paid before," she said removing the money from his hand before heading inside to pay for the gas. As she walked away, she spun around and did a little two-step, then looked over her shoulder smiling at him.

"Beautiful," he mouthed in silence.

She signed, "You are too," back at him.

"Hey get me a bottled water," he requested. She entered the Quick Stop and walked around looking for bottled water in the cooler. She picked up a magazine; on its cover was a picture of Tiffoni's Dad being pinned with his first star. Tiffoni's Mother and Brother were behind him, but she didn't see Tiffoni. "She wasn't there on purpose, I bet," Areesa thought to herself as she tucked the magazine under her arm, to show to Antonis. She found the cooler with the drinks. As she slid the glass door open, Antonis walked up behind her and wrapped his arms around her waist. Surprised, she dropped the magazine. Antonis tried to catch it, but it fell to the floor with the cover facing up.

"Oh man, look who's on the cover."

"Yea, I know. But who don't you see."

"Please tell me *that Private* didn't miss her father's important day."

"Ok, I won't tell you."

"What's up with her? You know she reminds me of an out of control brat."

"She comes from money, maybe that's why."

"Money?"

"Yea, old money," Areesa said walking away from the cooler as Antonis followed behind her shaking his head up and down, looking at the cover, understanding.

"So what's up with your girl? You know when I Buddied you two up, I did it hoping you two would balance each other out. Check this out, before she got to us, the Drills said she was a trip . . . they even implied she failed her PT test on purpose. It seemed to have worked 'cause you sure have gotten pushy girl," he said smiling at her.

"Umm. You know Antonis, when Tiffoni turns twenty-one she'll inherit over a million dollar trust fund set up by her grandparents for the first born grandchild in the their family."

"Get out-of-here?" he said, never knowing anybody personally or otherwise clocking like that. "So why is she in the Army?" he asked confused. "I tell you what if it was me, I wouldn't be in nobody's military. Her family is whacked."

"Antonis, that's not a nice thing to say. Where are we going?"

"Well I have an old friend at a Fort about another thirty minutes down the highway. I thought we'd stop by, say hello and have lunch down there. And, hey there's a great park at the bottom of the peak I want you to see."

"Have you ever been there before . . . with people?" she asked. He knew her question was loaded, and it made him feel good that she was concerned like that.

"Yea, but not the way you're thinking." His answer made her smile. She didn't want to go any place he had previously been with another female.

They went through the front gate of the Fort. "Awe, yea, I remember this building, it's where a friend of mine lived. Uh-oh where did that come from?"

"What?" she asked.

"Those barracks weren't there when I was here."

"Yea... they were. You're just lost. It's ok, if you are, you just have to be willing to admit it," she laughed.

"Lost. Nooo, lost I'm not. I use to live here. I know this place like I know . . ."

"What? please don't say the back of your hand. Many of men have gotten lost and stayed lost because they knew the back of their hand."

"Oh, oh . . . I see where you're going, you think I'm lost. Look, over there . . . there's, that's the uh, uh . . ." Areesa giggled as he attempted to refresh his memory. After about ten minutes, he decided to back track. Areesa sat quietly with a smile of her face. Whenever he glanced over at her, she would look straight ahead trying to conceal her amusement at his predicament. He finally stopped a soldier who was walking down the one-way street they were on to ask for directions. As the soldier pointed, it was as if a light bulb went on. He realized that a club he use to hang out at was now a Company Orderly Room. "That's what's throwing me off," he contended and Areesa laughed at him, while rubbing his left shoulder. Antonis put the car in drive and drove right to his friend's barracks.

He introduced Areesa to his friend. "Yea man, what's up with West? he finally had enough of the trail."

"Yea, I guess." As his friend talked about being a drill sergeant Antonis looked over at Areesa, and smiled at her. He felt proud introducing her to one of his oldest friends. He thought she was attractive when he first met her, but it wasn't until she was sitting across from him did he realize, how girly, lady like she was. She fitted in, no matter what the surrounding, what she was wearing, or who she was talking to, she was very comfortable to be around. They sat in his room and talked for about an hour. She just listened in on their conversation nodding her head understanding what they were saying about the routines of military life. When asked how long she had been in, she only said not long, and Antonis laughed. He made her a promise he would not tell anyone she was still in training. She wondered if Antonis was closer to Drill Sergeant West or this guy or maybe they were all friends since she heard Drill Sergeant West's name come up a few times.

Antonis asked his friend about the location of the park the *Fellas* hung-out in during the summer a few years ago when he was temporarily stationed there. His friend told Areesa about the summer nights they used to park their cars near the stream, and laugh and talk as they listened to music while playing dominos and cooking on their grills. "It was all good," he hinted to let Areesa know it was in good fun. She graciously accepted what he was trying to get across to her, that Antonis was a sincere guy, kinda corny in a cool way. They said good-bye to his friend and headed for Antonis' park.

As they approached the park, the once distant mountain towered over them. Antonis made a left turn onto the graveled road that dead-ended in the park. Areesa gasped as the SUV swayed and rocked before coming to a halt. She stepped out of the SUV, overcome by the majestic Pikes Peak. She swung her door open, before Antonis could come around and open it for her she was out deeply inhaling the smell of the clean mountain air. Antonis leaned against the SUV, watching her, which he enjoyed doing. He took her by the hand and led her to a wooden gazebo nestled at the foot of the huge charcoal picturesque mountain. Beautiful lush green giant oak and pine trees filled the serene landscape adorned with randomly placed picnic areas and running trails that encircled the park. They sat under the gazebo and watched children play on the multi-color playground. Areesa put her right hand above her eyes to block the sun as she watched some of the older children throw small rocks in the stream that ran through the center of the park. Antonis pointed out to her where he use to run every morning, like the two soldiers running across one of the narrow wooden bridges that connected the two sides of the park.

"What do you think?"

"It's so beautiful, Antonis . . . it's so beautiful," she whispered.

"I'm glad we're here."

"Me too," she said. Areesa biting her bottom lip, and then sighing told Antonis something was wrong with her. Not even the beauty of the surroundings and fresh air could keep her mind off the past couple of days. He sat patiently waiting for her to share her thoughts. "I tell you what, that Stryker had everybody fooled. Didn't she?" Areesa let out a hearty laugh. "What are you thinking about?" Areesa didn't respond, instead she laughed aloud at his words about Tiffoni, because he was right.

"You know, Tiffoni knows most people think she's a brat who intentionally does things to pull their strings. I think she gets a kick out of seeing people's expression when they find out who her Dad is too. And she loves embarrassing him."

"I bet she does," he said laughing, "Areesa, did you ever talk to Addie again?"

"Yep."

"Are you going to try working things out with her?"

"Yep."

"So how much longer are you going to stay here?"

"I'm leaving a few days after you. Addie invited us to dinner at her house. Do you wanna go?"

"Yep," he said mimicking her short response. Antonis went back to the SUV to get the food they purchased earlier. Together, they laid a blanket on the ground. As Areesa sat down on the blanket, she hoped Antonis would not want to talk about her parents or Addie anymore. They ate their food and talked about everything except her situation, which was fine with Areesa. After they finished eating, they strolled through the park playfully enjoying each other while holding hands. They paused near the stream and sat on a weather worn bench and talked, opening up their hearts to each other, sharing hopes, disappointments, and dreams. He sat on the edge of the back of the bench and she sat between his legs, throwing rocks into the stream.

"Antonis, how did you end up in the Army? I mean what's your story? Everyone has one. Besides you've seen me at my worst . . . I hope. There's so much I don't know about you."

"Yea, I know. Well, my Moms raised my sister and me by herself. My Pops was killed on the streets. It was hard back then especially since I was a hardheaded boy. She did the best she could in spite of welfare, a run down apartment, drugs, gangs and my Pop's death. Moms had to deal with all of that and a lot of heartache from me. I was in and out of ju-vie. A few months before my eighteenth birthday I got caught in the wrong place with the wrong crowd and ended up getting arrested along with everybody else. After the cops ran my name through the system, saw I was on probation and I was breaking the neighborhood curfew, I was locked-up all night. My Moms wouldn't come and get me . . . she was tired Areesa. I took her through so much. It hurts my heart, when I think about all the changes I put her through. Talking back, lying, stealing, not wanting to do anything around the house, always getting in trouble in the 'hood, hanging with the wrong dudes, coming and going when I wanted, just barely making it in school. To say my attitude was bad is an understatement. So, this Judge, the first black judge I had ever seen . . . I thought yea he's not gonna do nothin', except give me a slap on the wrist and send me home. Wrong. Old boy sat up there on his bench like a black king on his thrown, looking down on me. He told me, I had two options. My first- jail. Girl I tell you, my eyes popped out of my head. You know how cartoon characters make those noises when they get slapped upside their heads, I heard the same noise, and unlike the cartoons my head was hurting." Areesa laughed. "Don't laugh girl, Ol' boy had me going, scared me. Jail. Me? I don't think so, I just wanted to look bad, I wasn't interested in being bad. Anyway, I held my breath waiting to hear my second option. I had already told myself whatever it was I was taking it. I-was-taking-it, and I wasn't ever coming back to another court house. Check this out, he said enlist into the

Army. I staggered back, stunned. I thought he was going to say community service or something like that. Naw, he said the Army. What's your choice, he asked." Areesa turned so she could see his face. "That man must have seen something in me, I hadn't seen in myself. He didn't give a long speech about how I was headed for the grave or what a disappointment I must be to my parents. All he said was I'm presenting to you life and death. So, which one are you choosing?" Antonis stated throwing his hands into the air.

"What did you say to him?"

"Thank you Sir, I'll do the Army. I did my first about face, and walked out the door. The next morning my probation officer took me to the recruiting station. After everything was put in writing, I came home and told my Moms. Areesa she cried. She cried all that day. The next day she held me so tight in her arms and cried some more. I'll never forget how she looked at me. In the mean time, I still had three weeks before I was suppose to leave, so I helped my Moms around that broken down raggedy apartment, cut a lot of ties and stayed near the house. My Moms finally looked and talked proud about me."

"Oh Antonis," she said as she kissed his right hand that rested on her shoulder.

"I did go back to see that Judge a few days before I left. At first they thought I was comin' to take him out," he said laughing. "He came out of his office, and he saw me. And Bho he remembered me." Antonis' voice cracked. "He told 'em, let the young man come in. That I wasn't gonna do no harm. Man, I tell you what, he changed how I viewed myself, he made me feel like I wasn't another dead-head thug. Judge Covington, told me how he was in the military, how enlisting changed his life. Telling me to enlist meant nothing, but showing me, through his life accomplishments that enlisting could change my life means everything. Yea, yea. We sat in his office and talked for over an hour. He asked me to write him once I got settled."

"Did you?"

"Yep, I sure do."

"Do?"

"At least once a month. He sits on the New Jersey, District Court now."

"If it weren't for him, we wouldn't be together," Areesa said. They sat on the bench and talked endlessly, about their childhoods, families, direction their military careers were headed, her finishing her education, and how he felt when he graduated with his Bachelor Degree in Architectural Engineer, and how demanding his master degree program was.

They stood up and embraced each other for long periods of time, laughing and enjoying their time together.

"I'm so happy. You make me feel lovely Antonis."

"Yea, you make me feel good too. It almost feels unreal. I can see us out here cooking out with friends, kids playing, interrupting us as we laugh and talk. Living life, a good life." Areesa didn't respond to what he said because her sense of family was no longer trustworthy. He kissed her and she lovingly returned his affection, then looking into his eyes amazed by the boy he was and the man he had become.

She looked away, feeling she wasn't enough for him because she had to many problems for someone like him, who had such a sense of himself. He walked up behind her and rested his chin on her head.

"What's wrong?"

"I was just thinking about all you've been through, the last thing you need is pitiful, mixed-up me in your life." Insulted by her comment he turned her around to face him. As he looked at her she felt the way she did when she first meet him in the Barracks, frightened.

"What do you think, you're not good enough for me? Yea, there's a lot I don't know about you. I may not have all the answers for you, but I tell you this- I don't pity you and I know you're not mixed-up! As long as we're straight with each other there won't be any problems to hard for us to handle," he said.

"You give me so much … I'm just trying to figure out what am I capable of giving you. I just don't want you to feel you have to be here. I can take care of myself!" she said stepping back from his towering frame.

"I never said you couldn't take care of yourself. But isn't it nice to know, someone is on your side?" She turned away without responding. She wrapped her arms around herself, gazing into the stream, wishing her life would flow away with it. He walked up behind her and pulled her closer, wrapping his left arm around her waist and his right arm around her shoulders. Deeply inhaling the smell of her hair, he sighed. He kissed her on the back of her neck. "Bho I love you," he whispered into her hair. The outside world seemed to slip away as his words lingered in her mind. "Areesa, I do. I love you."

"Antonis, please. I know us being here together in this beautiful, peaceful place turns moments like this into a castle in the sky, but I don't expect for you to say you love me. You don't have to say that." He gently tightened his hold around her body with his eyes closed. He did not anticipate her responding the way she did, yet he knew for sure that he was in love with her. When she tried to pull away he loosened his hold on her. "Don't. Don't pull away. I know you're on an emotional roller coaster that's made you protective of your feelings and how you handle people."

"Yea, I am. So, don't you see, I can only end up hurting you, Antonis."

"What do you expect Areesa?"

"Trust and honesty."

"I will give you that. I promise that's what you'll have . . . we'll give it to each other. And believe me, my emotions are not driving me. It's the moments, days we've spent together. For the first time in my life, I'm someplace I haven't been forced to be. I had to learn the ways of streets if I wanted to survive. My Moms . . . yea, she did what she could with what she had, but I still had to take care of me, because I had no choice. The Army was not at the top of my career list. If Justice Covington hadn't forced me in, I wouldn't be here. I'm here with you because it feels like the most natural thing I've ever done. I don't wanna see you hurt. I don't wanna see you doin' without, but I do wanna give you all that I have."

"Antonis that's what my mom thought about my Dad, that he would make everything right for her, for us. But, look at me. I'm not alright. Right now I don't feel right... good inside unless you're with me. Something is wrong with that . . . I should feel good about me, for myself. I'm not going out like that. I want to bring more than a shattered person to the life we would share. I want, no I need to know who I am. And this isn't about finding my biological father, it's about finding me. What do I really like? What can I endure because of decisions I make, that are not a result of what my parents did? I don't know, I might like living in the city or having friends over to just hang out," she said holding her palms out, "or I might enjoy being alone because it gives me comfort, and not protection. But how will I know if I let you and Addie make everything ok for me? Your love, is more than I can ask for right now. I want to tell you I love you right now, this instance. But the words," she said caressing his face, ". . . the words may sound good, but they'll have no real meaning, and too many conditions. They'll just be words said on a beautiful cold day in a magnificent park. I know there's more for us than that," she said as tears rolled down her face. He looked into her brown oval eyes desiring never to see tears flowing from them. They were too beautiful. He wiped her tears away and then held her cold moist brown face in his hands. He shook his head up and down as he pulled her face close to his. She willingly submitted to the warmth of his hold, and embraced Antonis as tight as she could. She held on to her treasure.

the inheritance

Driving back to Denver wasn't awkward, but quiet. They agreed to meet in Areesa's hotel lobby at 6 p.m. and then drive to Addie's estate for dinner. Before getting out of the car, they kissed. Areesa hurried up to her room because she only had about two hours before he would be back to pick her up. Her laundry was on her bed, neatly folded in a clear bag next to her dry cleaning. She opened the bag, removing undergarments, and then she went into the bathroom to take a shower. She stayed in the shower for fifteen minutes. After blow-drying her hair, she brushed her teeth and put together four different out-fits at the same time. Finally, she settled on a clingy black ankle length sleeveless spandex dress that sensuously hugged all of her curves and a beige cashmere shall that belonged to her mom. She stood in the bathroom mirror checking out the way she looked and felt in the dress. All she needed to do was add finishing touches like silver jewelry and curls. She looked at her broken curling irons, realizing there was no hope for them, so she pulled her hair up into a French roll, leaving strands of hair falling in her face.

Once she was done, she liked what she saw. Pausing she realized how days ago she felt broken; emotionally, physically, and spiritually, now here she stood excited about seeing Antonis, a gift given at a party she never expected to have. Time was healing her and she felt strong and comfortable with her place in the world, strangely she thought, "this is me," a measure of self-reliance, something new, very new to her. She wished things were not as they were, yet she found wisdom in what her Mom often told her, "With every new second, minute, hour, day, a chance presents itself to do and be who you were created to be." Areesa realized her mother had a lot of wisdom and she was finally beginning to understand why. Having dinner with Addie, was the beginning to finding out what happened to her biological father, and her Mom and Dad. It was time. She was optimistic, that maybe her mom was right about him, Rowan, that he had changed with time. If so, then she could have the peace her parents never had. Before calling Antonis to pick her up, she called Tiffoni who was still in Chicago.

"What's up Buddy," Areesa said, as Tiffoni happily screamed into the phone. Areesa held the phone away from her ear, delighted by Tiffoni's exhilaration. Tiffoni was still Tiffoni.

"Where are you? I'm so glad you called Areesa. I'm missing you!"

"I'm in Denver," Areesa said in a hushed tone, because she knew Tiffoni was going to trip about knowing where she was.

"Denver? What Denver? My Denver? Who do you know in Denver? No, no . . . why didn't you tell me you were going to Denver? What's up with that?" she said without taking a breath.

"Nothing. I'm just hanging out with Sergeant Patterson, and I'm…"

"Sergeant who? Get out! Don't even go there with me, Areesa."

"Ok."

"Ok? Girl you'd better get to spilling your guts, and talk to me quick! What is going on?"

"Wait, wait Tiffoni. It's not what you think."

"Not what I think? Correct me if I'm wrong, but you're in my city with one of the finest Drill Sergeants I've ever seen and it's not what I think? Girl I think you need to get your head examined or a clue . . . quick, fast and in a hurry. Because if it was . . ."

"Tiffoni, will you please stop, and get out of my business, and your mind out of the gutter," Areesa teased.

"Did you sleep with him?" Tiffoni asked.

"Oh, no you didn't … I can't believe you went there."

"So you didn't, uh?" So was that his red Navi?"

"Yea, it is."

"How much longer are you guys going to be there?"

"He's leaving tomorrow."

"Sooo . . . what's his name."

"You sound as bad as I did when I asked him. It's Antonis."

"Say his name, say his name," Tiffoni sung, because Areesa said his name so smoothly.

"An-ton-is, Antonis Keith Patterson," Areesa replied in the same melody.

"Oh you should hear you, girl." They both laughed and giggled.

"Tiffoni you're a trip," Areesa said laughing. "Earlier today we hung out, and he took me to this park near the Fort. . ."

"Pikes Peak, or players park," Tiffoni said laughing.

"It's not even like that . . ."

"You're hooked? So when are you going to give-it-up?"

"It's not about all that. I care about him … he cares about me, Tiffoni."

"Areesa I'm just teasing. I hoped you two would get together. I knew he wasn't going to do nothing during Basic, too proper, military, formal, ceremonial …"

"Yea, yea, yea, I get it, enough, and he's nothing like you imagine," she said smiling.

"I'm glad you two hooked up. Actually, I was worried about ol'boy, I figured after Basic he'd get in touch with you."

"Yea," Areesa said looking down at the floor.

"Oh, don't go getting all sad on me. Enjoy your stay in my city, with one of the finest men I've ever seen."

"I will. Thanks Buddy. I'll talk to you later."

"You're welcome, Buddy."

They hung up the phone. Areesa gathered her coat and purse, and left her room to meet Antonis, while Tiffoni gazed out her hotel window. She was happy for them. After about ten minutes, she picked up the phone and called the Concierge. "Can you get me a late flight to Denver?"

"I'll check into it Ms. Stryker."

"Yes, do that as I pack," she said before hanging up the phone. "I belong in Denver, where all the excitement is."

Areesa did tell Tiffoni some of what was going on and Tiffoni was being extremely sensitive and supportive. Twenty minutes later, Tiffoni called Areesa to let her know she was flying in. Tiffoni told her, she was coming so she and Antonis would have someone to take them to the airport when it was time for them to leave. Areesa wasn't sure that was the whole truth, because Tiffoni was so unpredictable at times. Areesa did make her promise, no antics. They said their good-byes and Areesa remained tickled about talking to Tiffoni as she watched Antonis drive under the hotel awning to pick her up for dinner with Addie.

As Areesa walked towards the SUV, she smiled as she brushed her hair up with her hand, thinking about how Tiffoni teased her about the way she said his name. Antonis put the car in park, and exited the vehicle. He walked around the rear towards her, smiling. She loved to see him coming. She could pick him out of a crowd just by the way he walked. She loved the way he walked, so much so, she wanted to slap him on his butt whenever he walked up to her. She dropped her head to hide her blushing. As he came closer, she walked towards him and entered his open arms, snuggling up to him. She cuddled him as he squeezed her, then she took in a deep breath of his smell, that always made her soul feel warm and affectionate. In her eyes, he was truly the best-looking black man she had ever seen. Being with him was important to her, more than he knew. She held on to her hope that she would someday be able to give him as much unconditional love as he was giving her. As he held her in his arms she thought about how she'd watch love stories and movies with happy endings and long for those happy endings for her life, not because she deserved it, or that she was more deserving, more special than someone else, but because it's beautiful, right, and good. Antonis kissed her check. He told her, as he held the door open for her, "I spoke with Addie, and she gave me directions to her house." He didn't mention to Areesa, that he enjoyed his conversations with Addie, nor did he reiterate he believed Addie genuinely cared about her well being. As they drove, chatting about their day, he clumsily asked Areesa, not to shut him out and she agreed, as she noticed how uncomfortable he was making his request.

They slowly approached the gated community. Antonis didn't speak, and Areesa looked around for the exit she used the night she fled on foot from the walled community. She focused in on two walk-in gates. She shook her head side to side, because she didn't remember finding her way through either gate. As they drove into the community, they realized they were a long way away from the projects Antonis grew up in, and the isolated little house Areesa lived in. Areesa continued scanning the neighborhood, still unable to recognize anything familiar. She intently gazed at each estate as they drove into the cul-de-sac where Addie's house sat centered on the circle.

"What's wrong?"

"Nothing looks familiar." He placed his hand on her left shoulder and gently massaged her tensed muscle.

"Relax. Was it light outside like this, or already dark?"

"Yea," she said relaxing, "it was dark already," Areesa sighed.

"It's ok. Just relax," Antonis said as they drove up to the forth house from the front gate entrance. "What is it she does?" Antonis questioned. Areesa shrugged her shoulders. "Is this the kinda money the Strykers have?" he asked, as he turned right onto the half-circled driveway circling a water fountain in the center of the lawn. Areesa shrugged her shoulders again, as he continued to drive straight towards a covered porch located on the right side of the house.

"More?"

"More," he concluded. He slowly brought the car to a complete stop. Antonis got out of the vehicle, walked around to Areesa's side, and then opened the door for her. She stuck her long legs out of the car. Antonis admired them.

"Girl I tell you what, you know you got a brotha goin'." Areesa smiled and winked at him as she took his outstretched hand.

"You are so handsome, and you know how to treat a girl."

"I try," he said jokingly as he closed the door. She held his hand tightly as they walked up the stairs onto the porch. Anna answered the door. She immediately took their things and placed them on a sitting chair in the foyer.

"Miss Areesa, Miss Meaks is running late. She asked that you forgive her and to make yourselves comfortable. She promises to arrive as soon as possible."

"Thank you Miss. Anna," Areesa said. As Anna turned to lead them to the Greatroom, they looked at each other, shrugged their shoulders and followed her. She lead them into a room with a high ceiling. Beneath a maple wood loft were windows revealing beautiful gardens and paths in the backyard. The room was complimented by two oversized Providence sofas, two sitting chairs adorned with ivory pillows and throw blankets draping the arms, surrounding a black rod iron glass top table, and varnished wood flooring completed the elegant room. As Areesa strolled around the room, an antique birdcage, as tall as she was, caught her eye. No birds were in it, it was too pretty for that. The cage was decorated with a beautiful floral arrangement identical to the chair pattern and stood in a corner in the back of the room. Antonis, walked up behind her, and took her hand, she followed him towards two large hutches that stood guard on each side of the glass patio door. Areesa loved the beauty of the room, and she felt perfect standing in it with him, as they embraced and quietly talked. He led her to the sitting area, where they quietly sat. Areesa picked up a beautiful picture book of the Rain Forest and thumbed through it, while Antonis leaned his head back on the chair and closed his eyes. The quiet was broken when Anna entered the room, offering drinks and announcing, "Miss. Meaks will be arriving shortly."

"Are you going to make this meeting easy for her?" Antonis asked as he looked around the room from his relaxed position.

"I don't know if I can. This is really hard. I'd rather be some place else, now that I'm here."

"You know, you and Addie have a lot to share. She can give you your past back, the real past, and you can share your memories of your parents with her. Don't you think that's worth having?" She didn't respond because Addie had came home.

Dressed in a navy blue tailored suit with beautiful gold buttons down the front of the jacket and matching shoes, Addie rushed into the house, calling for Anna. As Anna approached her, Addie was anxiously twisting her ring around her finger. "Yes, Miss Meaks?"

"Are they here?" she asked as she stroked her hand across the back of her tapered feathered haircut.

"Yes, Ma'am. They are waiting in the Greatroom. Would you like for me to put these things away?" Addie glanced over at the half-oval shaped table where her briefcase and keys laid.

"Yes, sweet Anna, would you please." She asked as she walked towards the room where Areesa and Antonis waited for her.

Her entrance gave Areesa an excuse for not responding to his question. Areesa immediately became nervous at the sound of her approaching. Antonis stood to his feet to greet her. She entered the room with her arms

121

outstretched, greeting them both with firm handshakes, then hugs, to Areesa's great surprise. Her liveliness made Areesa smile, as she watched her move around the room explaining why she was late. Areesa secretly accepted her as her father's sister. Besides she thought to herself, they looked so much alike she couldn't deny it anymore. Addie took a seat on the sofa. As Areesa watched her move and talk, with her hands, she thought Addie looked like a giant sitting on small pieces of furniture.

Areesa's anxious feelings were aroused when Addie talked about sharing newspaper clippings about her biological father and his family. "You know Areesa you may want to visit with them while you're here."

"They still live here? Here in Denver?"

"Yes, Sweetie." The conversation became a backdrop to an overpowering sense of betrayal towards parents, if she met any of them. Addie and Antonis carried on the conversation, as she searched her heart, trying to figure out what her parents would want her to do.

"Your home is fantastic," Antonis said.

"Thank you Honey. I'll take the two of you for a walk around the grounds after dinner." Anna came in to let them know dinner was ready.

"Thanks Anna," Addie said as she stood. "Oh, Anna we'll have coffee," she looked at Antonis and Areesa for approval, "and tea," Areesa nodded her head up and down, "in here after dinner." Antonis stood and reached his hand out towards Areesa. "Oh, Sweetie, he's delightful, and you two make a stunning couple," she said as she lead them into the dinning room. Antonis winked at Areesa, and she snuggled up close to him, as they followed Addie out of the Greatroom.

Antonis pulled out Addie's seat at the head of the table, then he walked around and pulled out Areesa's chair to the left of him. Addie and Areesa locked eyes as Antonis stood between them. Addie subtly bowed her head in gesture to Areesa, that she means her no harm. Areesa accepted, as Antonis waited for them both to sit.

"Areesa I'm so glad you're here. And Sergeant Patterson it's a delight to have you in my home. Please eat, fill yourselves, then we can take a walk through the garden."

"Please, call me Antonis."

"What an unusual name. Are you of Spanish descent?" Addie asked.

"Yes Ma'am, my great grand-father was Hispanic. I carry the name of my uncle who was killed during the Korean War."

Areesa sat quietly, listening to them. She was trying, desperately, to fight off the "green monster" of jealousy as she watched them getting along so well. "Cool it, girl. Stop tripping," she thought to herself.

Addie told stories from the past about her parents, while they waited for Anna to bring them books from Addie's library. The more Areesa heard stories about her parents, especially the funny ones about how her Dad when he was a little boy, the more she relaxed.

"Charlie and I laughed all the time as children. He would laugh so hard sometimes, he'd cry. That always made our Momma mad. She'd say boy, you'd bettah stop laughin' like that. Cause if you pee in yo pants, I'm gonna whip you. See if you thank that's funny." They all laughed. "Your Father laughed, but he was a visionary too. Oh, how he wanted to make a difference in our old neighborhood. During High school, he wrote an essay about our neighborhood being comparable to a third world country. And, your momma, I tell you what, she was the first one ready to make a sign and pick-it. You know she was our school president during our junior and senior years in highs-school. Areesa did you know your mother was a rebel and your father a man of words?" She half smiled about the revelations, but she felt sorrow because she never heard him burst into laughter. Occasionally he smiled ... calmly ... momentarily. Yet it warmed her heart to know her Mom was out spoken, not this timid mousy woman afraid to go into an open field by herself. Antonis felt Areesa reaching for his hand under the oval eight-chair table. He held her hand and squeezed it. Without looking at him, she smiled.

Coming to spend time with Addie was turning out to be a good thing. She was boisterous, but genuine and caring. "Areesa, tell me how do you like the Army?" Addie asked. Antonis threw his head back smiling and shaking his head at the same time. She pinched his arm playfully, as Addie smiled at their easiness with each other.

"It's ok," she said covering Antonis' mouth with her hand.

"Do you know you have an uncle and two cousins in the Army?"

"No I didn't," she said smiling, "until a few months ago, I was totally alone in the world. This is all mind boggling," she said surprised by Addie's announcement. "What are their names?" she asked. Antonis attempted to speak, but Addie's excitement, drowned him out.

"Oh, yes . . . you have an uncle, Colonel, oh, let me correct myself, Brigadier General Stryker and . . ."

"Who? *The*, General Stryker? Just promoted General Stryker?" Areesa asked stun, completely blown away as she held her hands to her chest.

"Areesa have you meet him?" Addie asked excitedly. Antonis sat quietly, starring at Addie, and Areesa starred at him as Addie described Tiffoni, down to her some-timie ways.

"Well, my Buddy," Areesa said still looking at Antonis, hoping he would say something, but she knew in her heart he wasn't, ". . . my Buddy during

Basic, her last name is Stryker," she said not taking her eyes off Antonis, "and her Father, Colonel, but recently General . . . "

"Did you see the magazine cover? That child didn't even show up for her Father's promotion . . ." Areesa faintly heard Addie speaking. She was focusing on Antonis' blank expression and discomfort.

"Sweetie, if your Buddy's name is . . ."

"Her name is," Areesa paused, afraid to say her name aloud. She took a deep breath, still starring at Antonis, "Tiffoni." He blanked and dropped his head. "Tiffoni Stryker," she said again.

"Well Sweetie, your Buddy is your first cousin . . ." Addie ranted on. Areesa was in disbelief unable to speak. Antonis reached over to remove the fork from her shaking hand. Addie didn't understand what was going on, as she watched Antonis pull Areesa away from the table.

"She didn't know Addie. I didn't get a chance to tell her," Antonis said in a hushed tone.

"Well, Sweetie, it's ok. I mean, it's nothing you could have known." Addie said. Antonis turned and looked at her, and she went silent.

"You knew didn't you Antonis?" Areesa asked, her voice trembling as tears filled her eyes.

"Yea. I figured it out when I talked to her earlier today. I thought it would be better if it came from your Aunt."

"How could you?" she yelled in his face jumping from her seat. "I thought you were on my side. You're as bad as they are. How could you not tell me? I thought I could depend on you, trust you! Why am I always the last to know . . . how could you . . . how could you Antonis? I thought you were on my side," she said running out of the dining room. Addie stood too, and her linen fell to the floor along with Antonis and Areesa's. He picked up all three cloth napkins and threw them on the table and went after Areesa. Addie calmly grabbed his arm. He patted her hand, then she let go, and he went after Areesa.

He found her pacing, furiously. He watched her moving back and forward, and wondered what was going through her mind. To keep from physically striking out she knew she had to move, not cry, cause it did her no good. She was tired of the drama, her parents left her with, to deal with all alone. She was so tired, she didn't know what to do, except move, just move back and forward, forward and back, just move before she took somebody's head off! She started walking halfway up, then back down the stairs. After about a minute of that, she started walking in circles in the foyer, frantically swinging her arms and hands. After a few moments, she turned and paced in the other direction, when she locked eyes with Antonis who was standing in the shadow of the foyer watching her. She turned and walked outside where she resumed her pacing in the cold night air.

"Areesa. Areesa, wait," he called out, but she kept pacing with her arms wrapped around her body in the middle of Addie's lawn, as Addie watched them from inside the foyer window. "Bho," he said grabbing her, she snatched away, "what's going on with you? Don't act like this. Come back inside so we can *all* talk." She looked at him, pulled away and went back to pacing. "Come on Areesa, stop acting like this, we're worried about you. Come back inside so we can talk." She wasn't listening. "Areesa. OK what do you want? Tell me right now, what you want? You have to stop reacting like this, it makes everyone upset . . . and I know by now you know, no one is trying to . . . to hurt you. I mean, so what if Stryker has turned out to be your cousin. What difference does it make!"

"Oh that's good Antonis. That's real good."

"Stop it! Ok, I made a bad call. I found out about Stryker when Addie was giving me directions to get to her house. Hell, I was as blown away as you are. She didn't know, I . . . that we knew them. She was just going on about you meeting your Uncle Charles Stryker, and his wife and kids. Then when she named the daughter, Tiffoni … you could have blown me over with a feather … I just thought how is she going to respond …. so, … I … "

"Don't you think it would've been better if I heard this from you? No better yet, let me tell you something. I'm hurting! I feel like my insides are leaking out of my body onto this lawn. I'm angry . . . I want to yell until I can't hear myself anymore! I'm hurting, Antonis."

"I know. I know you are, but I'm asking you to let go of your hurt. Bho, come with me. Come back inside with me. No more has to be said about them. I'll tell Addie you only want to hear more about your parents, then it'll be done, you . . . then we can walk away from here and go on with our lives . . ."

"Go on with our lives?"

"Yes. *Our* lives. Yours, and mine. We can walk away together."

"I'm not walking away from anything! No," she said shaking her head side to side, in disbelief. "No more running. Yea, you are right. It will stop here. I'm tired of being the one destroyed by a past beyond my control. You wanna know something Antonis, contrary to popular belief, I'm not some china doll who needs to sit in her pretty box high on a shelf, only taken down for an occasional dusting. I'm human, and I'm suffering because of decisions made before I was even born. But you want to know what's really wild about this? If my parents had lived I still wouldn't know about them, or you."

"Areesa, don't…"

"Am I so different from everyone else that I shouldn't expect basic honesty and trust in my life?" she asked pointing at her heart, "I am the same as Addie,

Tiffoni, my mom and dad. I need it too. Remember that Antonis," she said, but he looked away. "No, look at me!" He looked into her eyes, "You said I've grown, that I've become stronger. So tell me Drill Sergeant, why didn't you have enough in YOU, for me tonight? To tell me... not just any ol' body, but Tiffoni, Antonis . . . Tiffoni is my cousin . . . ," she cried.

"What difference does it make? It doesn't change who we are and what we mean to each other. Don't you get that? What your parents did doesn't have to change us and what we have," he said starring into her eyes.

"It has ... it makes a difference! Why are you pretending that if not for their lies, we wouldn't know each other."

"But we do, why can't you accept us, and what we have?"

"Tell, me . . . please tell me when do I get to decide what I want, what I should hear and know? When Antonis . . . when do I get to say IT MAKES a difference and, everyone accept it does because I said it does!" she screamed. He didn't respond as they stood toe to toe. "Who are you, and for that matter Addie, or my parents to decide what kind of life I should have? You know, all of you are full of answers, but all the wrong answers. I'm telling you I'm not taking it anymore," she said screaming at him. "I won't accept any one else interfering in my life. It's my life and I'm going to live it the way I want."

"What about love Areesa? What about wanting to stand by you no matter what or who comes and goes in your life?"

"Love? Isn't that what I've been getting? I don't know what love is anymore." He looked away from her. "But I do know this, I've got to learn to survive anyway I can right now, surely you can understand that."

"Bho, you don't mean that. Come with me back into the house. We can work this out."

"No, you go . . . I'm through talking. It's time to go after what's rightfully mine."

"What about us Areesa?" he asked, his eyes appearing glazed, as he rubbed his right hand down the back of his head.

"It's not going to work," she said. The words took her breath away, yet she knew she couldn't take them back. As she stood in the center of the lawn waiting for him to speak, her body felt numb, as the darkness concealed her tears. "I need someone who's on my side."

"But I am . . . you gotta know that."

"No, not anymore," she said shaking her head, "I can't forgive you for this. When I needed trust the most you let me down."

"Baby ... please, try and understand . . . I just wanted to protect you. It's all I've ever wanted," he said reaching out for her, but she backed away from him. He reached for her again this time securing her upper arms in his grip. A light rain began to fall on them as they gazed into each other's eyes.

Starring into his eyes rushed pain into her heart causing her to gasp for air, and she knew for now he was lost to her, in spite of an unspoken knowing that she was connected to him in a way that nothing could ever destroy.

"I know you're hurting . . . I'm hurting too, I know you know my heart, it longs for you. I wish I could turn time back, and change the past hour, but I can't. And right now, looking into your eyes, your eyes. Standing here with you, touching you, knowing you're safe," he said holding his head back as the light rain gently washed his face, "I know for now I have to let you go. Is that what you want? Do you want me to let go?" At the sound of his words the memories of their moments in time flashed before them; first day at Basic when they first meet, the night on the balcony, Graduation day, his office, the club house kitchen, his room, dinner, her room, their drive, the park . . . their park, his touch . . . her touch. Her silence was his answer. "Always remember us . . . that it was all good . . . it was good Areesa. Don't ever forget how strong you are . . . I won't." He pulled her close, and she rested her body in his arms. She closed her eyes and inhaled, absorbing their memories into her mind and heart.

"Good-bye Antonis," she said slowly withdrawing herself from his grasp. She backed away still facing him. A part of her wanted to stay with him and leave Denver. But the other part of her, the need to know what happened to her biological father, and why her parents' honor was taken away from them, was stronger.

As she turned and walked away from him, she counted the six steps up to Addie's porch. She stood under the porch lights watching him walk across the lawn.

Addie watched them from inside. She wanted to interfere, but she didn't. She felt helpless watching them walking away from each other.

Areesa came inside. She and Addie stood rooted in their spots, watching Antonis get into the SUV, back down the drive, and drive away.

"I'm going to find out why my parents ran like animals for their lives. I've been deprived of my true identity and the only man I'll ever love . . . and when I find out who is to blame, they will pay. They will pay."

it's like that now . . .

Areesa sat silently for what seemed like hours. She kept thinking about how far he was from her. Initially she wanted to run after his SUV, but she didn't, because she didn't know who would be running after it to get in it. "Let him go, let him go," she said to herself repeatedly. To drown out her pain, she allowed her mother's voice to flow through her mind. "There's a time for everything, and a season for every activity under heaven … there's a time to tear down and a time to build and a time to love and a time to hate … always know things happen for a reason Areesa. That's what Ecclesiastics says."

"Oh, Mommy, I'm so lost, so confused, what do I do, please tell me what to do," she cried. Then she felt her mother's presence holding her, reminding her to take action as if everything depended on her, and pray as if everything depended on God. Areesa's heavy sorrow, revealed her season of tearing down and hating. It was difficult for her to believe a time to love and build would follow. For now, she cried for him, because it was too hard to see the sun when she was trying to find shelter from the storm.

Areesa was emotionally over stimulated. She realized she was the shadow of the child her mother called *Ariisa,* a rising star that somehow had fallen victim to decisions made on her behalf over twenty years ago. She laughed at the notion of it all. No one could have predicted the impact all of this was going to have, not just on her anymore, but Tiffoni too. Their lives were never going be the same, now that she knew their truth. Areesa shook her head no, placing her head on her knees, while rocking them side to side. She sat quietly, absorbing she and Tiffoni were cousins and that she would probably never see Antonis again. She needed relief, she felt like running to the ends of the world. If such a place even existed she didn't know, she just wanted to go there. She wanted to reach out and do the impossible, because the idea of being a Stryker, was the last thing she ever expected to hear from anybody, it was so far fetched. After awhile Addie came and sat on the stairs with her. They simply sat in silence for several minutes, looking around the spacious foyer, but never at each other.

"Tell me about Ro, Rowan? Am I saying it right?"

"Yes. Rowan was the youngest and the wild child. Your grandmother adored him, he could do no wrong in her eyes, but your grandfather wished he would get a job … you know. He saw your Mom one night when we were hanging out, he never stopped bothering her until he had her . . . and your Mom, well, hey she welcomed his attention."

"Did he love her?" Areesa asked closing her eyes and holding her breath at the same time. Addie looked at her face as she sat on the stair rocking back and forth. She made a conscious decision to tell the truth, because the truth was all they had to build on.

"Honestly, I don't know. It would surprise me if he didn't. Anyone who encountered your Mom, loved and respected her. I think if he wasn't so weak minded, you know selfish, irresponsible, lazy ..."

"I get the picture," Areesa added.

"He could have. But I think he just didn't know how to love someone else, you know what I mean, it's hard to give when you're always expecting to be given to."

"Thank you, Aunt Addie," Areesa said. Tears swelled in Addie's eyes, at the unexpected words.

"For what Sweetie?"

"For telling me the truth. So what about the General, what's the story behind his commission?"

"Your guess is as good as mine on that one. He was expected to walk the narrow path. I was shocked when he was commissioned into the Army too, though it worked out for me, because I took his position with their firm. You know the firm is a Fortune 500 Cooperation with stocks and diverse holdings."

"Is she, Tiffoni like her dad? Sounds like they are more alike than they realize."

"Maybe so . . . maybe so, because he didn't have to join. He had finished his degree, and it was expected that he would run the Denver Office for his family. But, to everyone's surprise he left a few weeks later."

Areesa and Addie sat on the stairs sharing more stories about Charlie and Ginny, as they looked through old school yearbooks and photo albums. Addie had one picture of Rowan sitting in a club and her Mom on his lap. Areesa smiled at the vision of her mom sitting on a man's lap, in a club, wearing make up, jewelry and a tight sweater and pen skirt. A feeling of sadness came over her for her father, because she never saw her mom that way with him. Yet, a conflicting feeling weighed her down with sadness. Amazingly, the woman she was becoming felt joined with the woman her mother was. After an hour or so, she told Addie, Tiffoni was coming, and she had agreed to meet her at the airport.

Addie offered her a car to drive, but Areesa preferred to take a taxi back to the hotel, then take the hotel shuttle to the airport. She and Addie hugged a long time as they stood in the foyer waiting for her taxi. Addie insisted again that Areesa either take one of her cars, or let her driver take her back into the city, but Areesa declined. As they waited Addie wanted to ask her about Antonis, but Areesa's taxi drove up. Addie placed one of her heavier coats around her shoulders because it had begun to lightly snow, then they embraced once more, and Areesa left. Addie stood on the porch, waving at her until she couldn't see the taxi anymore. Anna came out and asked Addie to come in. "Anna, there she goes . . . that child is her mother. I know she's going after answers, and that money. I didn't know there was an inheritance and I know for sure Virginia and Charlie didn't."

Areesa, wished she could talk to Antonis, she wanted to confess to her Aunt how much she was missing him, instead she settled the confusion between her mind and heart; she knew they would never have the future they talked about in the park. During the drive, she concentrated on words she could use to tell Tiffoni they were first cousin. "It would be nice not to have to bare this burden alone any more. Still, too many questions. I'd better not say anything," she thought. She wondered why Tiffoni never mention him … Rowan. Areesa talked out loud to herself, "Maybe she doesn't know about him, since he died before she was born? Too many questions. Still too many questions. I'm not going to say anything." The inheritance suddenly came to the top of her thought list. "Let's see, I'm July. She's May . . .," she held up both hands, "August, September, October, November, December, January, February, March, April, May. Ten months too late, Tiffoni." Realizing Tiffoni was her only way to get next to the family without revealing who she was, she knew Tiffoni had to remain in the dark until the time was right. She arrived back at her hotel and an hour later in a different outfit, she took the hotel shuttle to the airport to meet Tiffoni.

Tiffoni was unaware that Areesa was coming. Areesa kept hearing what General Stryker said when he was at their graduation party, about them looking alike around the eyes. Areesa wanted to see, to look in Tiffoni's face and see if she saw herself.

She stepped off the hotel shuttle into wispy snow and hawking wind blowing and whistling causing her hair and coat to flap wildly. She rushed towards the double class doors that automatically opened for her. She stepped inside the terminal, and a gush of warm air pushed against her. Looking around for an arrival monitor, she brushed her hair out of her face, and shook snow off her coat. Spotting the arrival monitored she walked towards it and scanned over it for Tiffoni's flight status, the only flight arriving from Chicago. She made her way through the corridors down the escalator to the luggage claim area. Areesa stood at the carousel, watching people coming and going. She saw herself bringing Antonis to the airport. It would have been excruciating standing there trying to say good-bye to him. Her eyes filled with tears. She looked out the windows surrounding the area she stood in, when her own reflection became more visible than everyone else's faces. She starred, hoping Antonis' would appear like all the other times he did when she needed him, without having to ask. She walked towards the windows, the closer she came, the more she searched for him outside the windows. Before she knew it she was so close to the window she could see her breath, and tears. She reached out, and wiped the tears off her reflection on the glass. Her head thumped against the image. "Cool it girl, folks are going to think you're nuts," she said. She took a seat and waited for Tiffoni.

Tiffoni lagged behind letting most of the passengers get off the plane. She was still angry because she couldn't get first class seating. Experiencing first hand what went on in coach was not a part of her impulsive plan: The man seated next to her nearly talked her to death to the point she wanted to throw him off the plane, he got on her nerves so bad. Several times the words sat on the tip of her tongue, to tell him to get out of her business and face, but she didn't because she could hear Areesa telling her, "Now Tiffoni, that's not nice." Once the plane landed, and it was ok for passengers to debark, he offered to get her bag down, but she smiled and told him, "No thank you." What she really wanted to say was, "Mister isn't talking me to death enough? Please don't worry about my bag." I've been hanging around Areesa to much she thought pulling her small travel bag down from the overhead compartment.

Areesa stood right at the opening of the tunnel waiting to see Tiffoni. Only a few more stragglers were still coming out, and behind them moving slow, was Tiffoni. The low lights in the tunnel gave her bronze complexion a soft glow making her face appear as perfect as a model on the cover of a magazine. As soon as she saw Areesa, she revealed her beautiful smile. Despite her ambivalence, Areesa followed her impulse to run and hug Tiffoni.

"Areesa what are you doing here?" she happily asked.

"I'm here to meet you, of course." Tiffoni gave her a doubting look. Then she looked around for Sergeant Patterson.

"Are you alone?"

"Yes, I'm alone. Hey this is our time." Areesa's willful lying had begun as she smiled looking into Tiffoni's eyes. They were her eyes, too. Shaking off what she saw, she pressed through her ambivalence about the betrayal she was releasing on her life. They walked arm in arm towards the spinning luggage carousel. A man in a black suit, with a white collared shirt and black tie, held a sign that read: Ms. Stryker. Tiffoni knew she had to ride coach, but the buck stopped there.

"Is he waiting for you?"

"He most certainly is? How do you think I'm getting …," she paused. "Areesa don't go there, girlfriend. When I'm in my city it's first class." After the gentleman retrieved her luggage and loaded it on the baggage trolley, he lead them to a snow covered black stretch limo parked in front of doublesliding doors. They walked arm in arm out into the night as Tiffoni told Areesa her horror story having to ride in coach, which made Areesa laugh. She talked about some man so bad that Areesa felt sorry for him, having to sit next to her. The driver held the door open for them, and closed the door once they were comfortably seated, then he placed Tiffoni's luggage in the trunk. Once inside the limo, he informed them about all the amenities for them to use at their leisure. They rode along the rolling slops of the highway on the outskirts of the city. In the far off distance, brilliant lights from the city lit up the black night. Tiffoni sipped on a raspberry sparkling water as Areesa watched the scenery flash by. Tiffoni talked about how much she loved Denver, even when it was cold, it was a beautiful place, because you expected the cold weather, in a matter of fact way she said, "People look forward to it." As she went on about how much she loved Denver, Areesa was silently asking for her forgiveness. She wasn't as good at deception as she thought she would be. "How do people do this?" she asked herself over, and over.

"Areesa what's so fascinating out the window? You know you're not fooling anyone except yourself. So what happened to Sergeant P? and please for heavens sake don't tell me some army emergency came up and he had to leave unexpectedly."

"Things go wrong you know. We don't have as much in common as I thought we did."

"You lie, and not well I might add."

"Tiffoni why didn't you show up for your Dad's pinning promotion?" Tiffoni pushed a button and talked to the driver, ignoring Areesa's question. She leaned back in her seat with her hands on her hip. She opened her mouth to speak, but nothing came out. She made jesters with her hands to explain herself, as Areesa watched in disbelief, Tiffoni squirmed and wiggled, then uttered, "Uh . . . uh, I-I, uh."

"Never mind Tiffoni. Is your brother still here?"

"I don't know. Areesa you should try this water it's really good. I'm going to tell Mom about it, she'll love it," she said, reading the brand name aloud.

"Tiffoni if it makes you uncomfortable to talk about it, I understand."

"No it's not that. I just didn't want to be there. My presence wasn't necessary. You know."

"Yea, I know. So how big is your family? I don't want anymore surprise. Like the President isn't a distant cousin or something?"

"No, the odds of you being in the family is greater," Tiffoni said laughing. Areesa sank into her seat. "Let's see. My Mother has two sisters and they have children. Her parents passed away many yeas ago. Grammy, died some years ago. And oh, yea my Dad's younger brother, Rowan was killed before I was born. My Gramps is still living." Areesa readjusted her body, then touched her chest. She thought her heart was stopping. Tiffoni said his name, Rowan. Shocked to hear his name come from her mouth, made the situation dreamlike. She shifted her weight on the black soft leather seat. "My Father doesn't talk about him much. My Mother on the other hand, when she gets mad at my Father she throws him up in his face. I remember one night during dinner, and this shocked me, but my Mother was teasing my Father about how Uncle Rowan always got *the girl*. If he hadn't been killed he probably would have gotten her too, like he did some woman name Vickie. Nooo, that's not it. Veronica. No, no, Virginia. Yea Virginia! She was the hot ticket back then from an old neighborhood, called the Lower End according to my Mother. My Uncle Rowan, the ladies' man that he was, was in love with her from what my Mother said, and it drove my Father nuts, because he liked her too. But my Uncle Rowan got *the girl*," she said giggling. "Areesa are you OK. Areesa, are you ok! Did you see something out the window? You look like you're going to be sick." Areesa had no idea Tiffoni running off her mouth would reveal so much. She wanted to tell her to SHUT UP, when she said her Mom's name. Like her Mom was some, some alley-bat, fast-tale girl to be caught. Areesa felt her flesh rise up. She wanted to tell the driver to pull the car over so she and Tiffoni could get out and fight. Throw down right there. In the dark, in the snow, on the side of the highway. Areesa kept taking deep breaths, as Tiffoni buzzed the driver asking him for a brown bag, because she thought Areesa was hyperventilating. Areesa waved her hand at Tiffoni to roll down the windows, while grabbing for her water. She took a big gulp. Tiffoni frantically tried to help her. After a few minutes, Areesa finally calmed herself down. She lightly patted her chest as the cold air blew into the limo tossing her hair around and cooling her body off. "Areesa are you all right? Girl are you trying to give me a heart attack?"

"That's funny. That's what I thought you were trying to do to me."

"What? Areesa what's wrong with you?" Tiffoni asked irked by her ridiculous comment. "Why would I want to give you a heart attack Areesa?"

"Lighten up Tiffoni, I'm Ok. Something must have gotten caught in my throat." Tiffoni sat back in her seat staring at Areesa, she had never seen anyone act like that. The driver asked how they were doion, and they both assured him everything was fine. They rode in silence until they entered the city limits. By this time, Areesa had composed herself and gotten a grip over her emotions. She asked Tiffoni to tell her more about her family. Tiffoni was a little hesitant, but Areesa assured her, she was feeling better. Tiffoni's tone was somber when she said, "You know, he *had* to be the head of the family, like my brother will eventually have to be. It doesn't matter how much he loves the military, and what he does. And they all know I won't let them force me into it, like he didn't let them force him into it.

"Your Dad?"

"NO, my uncle. My Mom tells me all the time that's why my Dad gets frustrated with me, because I'm doing my own thing like my Uncle Rowan did. My Dad is good at letting people know that loyalty is everything."

"Is that such a horrible thing?"

"In my family, if you don't support the name out in public as a united front then you're not loyal. We're like a group of females. If one doesn't like someone, then we all must follow suite. Regardless, of what we think as an individual."

"Is that why you didn't show up for his pinning?"

"What do you mean, I couldn't get a flight out, that's why I wasn't there?"

"You came here," Areesa winced. Tiffoni remained silent. "It's like, sense our arrival you act like money. When we were in basic, you were always trying to act like you came from a struggle. That had to really piss your Dad off."

"Areesa, you maybe older than me, but you haven't lived as much life as me."

"How much could you have lived Tiffoni? I don't get it with you."

"Really. What do you know? Oh yea, you think because of my family's name, the worst I can expect out of my day is what? Spilt chocolate milk on my pink petticoat dress, and I have to change into a white one at the most inopportune time, like playtime, or better yet, I go in a store and get what I want because I don't have to worry about the price tag. My family has money Areesa, but money doesn't have me."

"No, I..."

"No is right. You don't know. Listen, my brother could never lead our family because he can't make tough decisions, like my Dad does. I can't be expected to do anything right in this family, because my father fears me, because I'm not loyal to an idea, but loyal to my own ideas and beliefs."

"What a mean thing to say about your father, he adores you."

"Sometimes my need to flaunt my independence in their faces, causes me to make bad decisions," she said sadly, "which, really only proves them right about me."

"I don't know."

"Oh, Areesa, you are as indecisive as my brother. So neutral."

"No, I'm not. So how did your grandparents feel?"

"After Grammy unexpectedly died, my father became the CEO. But he had already been commissioned. Her death affected his political ambition and military superstardom. Trying to get, and keep, a president for the firm, hindered his first year of military life. He almost gave up his commission, which would have made my Mom, ecstatic."

"So what did he do?"

"Well Gramps stepped in for a while, but he knew he wouldn't be long, cause it was Gammy that kept it all together. He was missing her, and really didn't want to be there on a daily basis." For a few more months, the firm went through Presidents like crazy. Get this, my Father wanted someone who would be loyal; not talking the talk, but walking in it. He understood the difference. He would drop in unexpectedly and turn the office out. It was crazy. If there was a negative news report or poor public relations he would fire people, send them packing." Areesa absorbed every word she spoke about the family, learning how Addie came in.

"So the solution was to get someone he could control?" Tiffoni glanced at her. A few minutes went by without words being spoken.

"No, I don't think control the way you see it, but control over the business without having to be told how to control. Does that make sense?"

"A little," Areesa said.

"Trusting someone who would be all of that came nicely wrapped in a statuette called Addie Meaks. You have to meet her Areesa. She's an extraordinary woman. My Grammy would have adored the strength and grace she has brought to the Firm. She has so many strengths, like business savvy, common sense, and she can make tough decisions, and changes. According to my dear mother, who doesn't have a secure bone in her body, Addie went from rags-to-riches. I remember sitting in my father's office suite, listening to my mother whine about why my Dad hired Addie for the president position. At first, I thought it was the green-eyed monster, but I think it was more than that. You know, they all came up together, from different sides of the track, but they all knew each other during high school. As a matter of fact, Addie was the first black woman I ever meet who wasn't related to me and she wasn't a maid."

"Really?"

"Yea."

"Wow."

"Once to get my Dad's attention, I tried to sell my stock. Addie bought it from me, so that it could stay in the family," Tiffoni laughed. "But that's the kinda of control he wanted in the firm. Someone he trusted, who would speak up, someone who would protect the family fortune."

They drove by Antonis' hotel, but Areesa didn't mention he was still in Denver, because Tiffoni would have wanted to stop and visit. Areesa didn't want that. Besides, she knew he wouldn't go along with what she was doing.

"My father is going to blow his stack when he sees me," Tiffoni confessed. "Areesa, I only came to Denver, because you're here."

"I know."

"I'm going to get some rest tonight. I'm staying at the Hilton. Then I'll go to Amethyst," Tiffoni paused to study Areesa's puzzled expression. "My parent's estate."

"You think another day is going to help you deal with him?" Areesa asked as the limo pulled up under the awning of her hotel.

"I don't know. Does it matter?"

"I think you need to answer that for yourself, Buddy."

"No. It doesn't matter," Tiffoni said as Areesa stepped out of the limo. She closed the door. Tiffoni slid over to where Areesa previously sat. Areesa watched the dark tinted window slowly come down. "I said no Areesa."

"I heard you. And, I don't believe you." Tiffoni pressed the window button, and the window ascended. Areesa looked at her until the window was up. The limo easily pulled away.

Areesa's thoughts were storming inside of her head as she entered the hotel lobby. She couldn't get up to her room fast enough. She wanted to call Addie. The phone was ringing as she entered her room.

"Hello."

"Have you heard from Antonis, Sweetie?"

"No. It's over Aunt Addie," she somberly said, "I'm letting go, he's letting go too. It's the right thing to do. Please try to understand, ok." Addie had great reservations about her decision, his too, but she didn't push the issue.

Addie confirmed much of what Areesa found out from Tiffoni, and she answered questions, Areesa didn't want to ask Tiffoni. Areesa had her answers. All that was left to do, was restore her parents' honor.

restored honor

Areesa awakened early. She looked over at the clock and knew Antonis was on his way to the airport, and that he would board his flight in a few hours. She sat up in bed, looking around the room for the telephone book. She fluffed and propped pillows up behind her after retrieving the telephone book from the nightstand drawer, and then she began to cry. She wiped her tears away with the back of her hands, and continued to thumb through the book. Occasionally, she looked out the window at the sky, still thinking of him, how much she missed him.

She wrote several telephone numbers and addresses down on a note pad. She leaned over and picked up her telephone to see if it was working. The dial tone hummed softly in her ear. She replaced the receiver and went to the bathroom. She kept sticking her head out, thinking she heard the phone ringing. She got into the shower. After about five minutes she got out, wet, and quickly stepped across the cold bathroom tile onto the carpet rushing towards the phone. She looked at the message button, and it wasn't glowing red. She stood silently as her wet hair dripped down her back, and her bare legs shivered, feeling an emotional struggle between willingness and unwillingness. Helplessly she starred at the phone wanting to hear his voice, but her will was set, she wasn't calling him, and she knew Antonis was not going to call her, out of respect for her wishes. Even though she knew this, she called the front desk asking if the phone in her room was working ok. She asked that her phone be ranged, just to ensure, one hundred percent that it was working. After the front desk rung her back, she sat on her bed and prayed for him: "Bless him with a safe flight, he's a good guy, a man's man. God let him know, I'm sorry I couldn't be what he needs right now. Watch over him and all he does ... protect him from the world, and from me too. Will You please, someday let him forgive me for choosing this path over his love for me. Let him remember us, all we shared as a good part of his life, and let me not forget too." After she prayed, she knew how much she did love him, and the idea of them.

Areesa left the hotel and headed for the library, which had an archive of local newspapers. What information she didn't find she found on the internet, especially information about the family firm. The information she discovered inspired her sixth sense, that urged her to go back in time, twenty years, and retrace the lives of her Dad and Rowan. Areesa went back to the neighborhood where her parents hung-out and the second floor apartment, on Quebec Street that her Dad lived in. She sat in her rental car, envisioning how painful it must have been for them to flee in fear. She wondered what the apartment looked like back then. What color it was when her parents lived in it. She wondered what was old and what was new. If they had the chance to visit, would they cry or laugh about old times. Would they have the courage to knock on the door and inform the tenants that they once lived there with their newborn child? She felt sorrow for what they had suffered and lost the night Rowan died, at the hands of his murderer. And Areesa knew *it wasn't her Dad.*

She started her car, thinking someone might become spooked about her sitting in front of the apartment building. She let the car run, but she didn't take it out of gear. She didn't want to go. In a weird and astonishing way, she felt connected to the apartment, the area, and her parents. So much so, she just simply wanted to stay put. She drew in a deep breath, and listened for her parents' voices, their scents, their touch, their undeniable love for her, her spirit joined with theirs, and once again, they were together as one. She gently pushed her turn signal down, waited for a passing car, then pulled into the driving lane as tears rolled down her face. She made her turns, automatically, back towards her hotel, occasionally she looked up at airplanes flying above her. Each airplane that passed over she wondered if it was the one Antonis was on. She still couldn't put him out of her mind.

She waved at the clerk as she passed through the hotel lobby. While waiting for one of the three elevators, she starred aimlessly at the beautiful fountain. The elevator came quickly. She arrived at her room, but before closing her room door, she removed her **DO NOT DISTURB** tag from the door. Once inside she looked around at all the papers and books she had gotten from Addie laying sprawled across the bed and desk. She sat down at the desk and called Tiffoni's room. She had already checked out. She looked around her room, and found another number for her.

"Hello."

"Listen to you, sounding all proper," Areesa teased in an English accent. Tiffoni laughed.

"Oh, you're trippin'."

"Now that's more like it. What's up?" Tiffoni began telling her about her unexpected arrival home, while Areesa felt heartbroken. She couldn't ignore the lump in her throat. She wanted to tell Tiffoni the truth, but the words wouldn't come out.

"So, how are things, truly?"

"Areesa, what's up with you? I just told you I came in this morning. My Mom doesn't know I'm in the house and my Dad isn't here yet. Are you coming over? I can send a car for you."

"Ok, I'd liked to come over later, and you don't have to send a car. Hey, it must be a pretty big house if your Mom doesn't know you're in it?" Areesa asked in a sober tone. A few seconds went by before either of them said anything.

"What's wrong? You don't sound like Areesa."

"Didn't you hear, I'm not. I'm a rising star."

"What? You're being weird again, so what's wrong? Something went on between you, and our favorite Drill Sergeant. Is he coming with you?" Areesa was silent. "Is he still here?"

"Sort of. I don't know Tiffoni."

"Is there anything I can do? You sound so sad."

"So much has happened since Basic, Tiffoni," she said holding her head backwards trying to stop her tears from falling. She put her hand over the receiver so Tiffoni wouldn't hear her sniffling, "No, there's nothing anyone can do. I just have to keep-it-movin'."

"That's a great idea. We'll both do it, keep-it-movin'." Areesa smiled as she wiped her tears away.

"What time should I be there? Not too early because I'm still a little tired." she said wiping her tears away.

"Well, anytime you want, I'm here. I can only imagine how it's going to go. My Dad is coming in tonight. You know you and my Dad have impeccable timing. He asked about you never calling is office. Wait until he finds out you came to Denver, without his approval, and funds."

"Really. Or maybe his real surprise will be seeing his daughter who he wished had been at his promotion. Maybe if you are agreeable he'll give you your inheritance and send you on your merry way."

"Two problems with that one Areesa," Tiffoni said. "He'll eventually get over my not attending the promotion and my Dad has no authority over my inheritance anymore, when the time comes it's mine. Whether he likes it or not, and that goes for everybody."

"So how's your mom and brother? Is he still in town?"

"No, he'll be back next week. Areesa if I didn't know any better, I'd think you were trying to feel my family out. Don't worry we don't bite." They both began to laugh for different reasons because Areesa knew by the time the evening came, and the sun rose in the morning they'd all want to take a big bite out of her. The two of them said their good-byes and planned for Areesa to arrive at the estate at about Seven O'clock.

"I hope they're ready. Because like it or not it's time to make what is wrong, right. I will restore my parents' honor, have my say, and get my inheritance. I hope you understand someday Tiffoni that I'm doing what I think is right," she said aloud as she sat on the side of her bed wiping away her tears, because she had no plans of ever crying about this again.

Areesa realized that once she arrived at the family estate there was no turning back. She called Addie to enlightened her about why she was going to the estate. She wasn't calling for approval, because she was going forward with her accusations without proof, but with a theory, and it didn't matter if Addie liked it or not. Anna answered the phone.

"Hi Anna, how are you this evening?"

"Fine Ms. Areesa, thank your for asking. I'll let Ms. Meaks know you're on the phone. Hold on please." A few seconds later Addie said, "Hello, Sweetie how are you?"

"I don't know yet, ask me in the morning."

"Oh, what's going on?"

"I just want you to know I figured out why Rowan wanted to take me from my mother and father."

"Are you sure you want to share this with me?"

"Mmm-umph. Did you know Rowan found out that the first born grandchild of the family was going to inherit a then half-million dollar trust fund?" she paused. "For the first time since my Mom told me, pleaded with me, to call you, I finally see the rainbow, outside this lonely storm I've been caught up in for so long," she said in a humbled soft voice. "Now I'm able to make sense out of what happened and why all of you acted the way you did. I'm sure none of you knew things would turn out this way."

"You're right. If you don't accept anything else from me, or your parents, know that we acted out of love for you. Maybe not perfect, but it was love and that includes Antonis too, Areesa." It was hard for her to speak about Antonis to anyone, so she didn't respond to Addie's comment about him.

"I'm struggling with emotions I never knew I had, Aunt Addie. I feel so principled sometimes, like right and wrong are crystal clear, but since my parents' deaths my principled ideas aren't clear, reasonable anymore."

"Sweetie, it's understandable that you feel these things. Do remember, that it's up to you where it all stops. Our fears and violence began all of this, but it will end only with your forgiveness." Areesa dropped her head, realizing everything was in her hands.

"I'm going to their estate at seven. Please, before you say anything, this is something I have to do. I'm not going to rest until I do. There are things you don't know. My Uncle, the powerful General. My distinguished and respected Uncle knows a lot more than he ever let on. The one thing he never counted on, was me turning up to claim what is rightfully mine."

"Areesa, you listen to me," Addie's voice was stern as she advised her, "he is a hard man. He is not someone to challenge during an emotional whirlwind. You must know who you're dealing with. Even if you think *he's* the cause of everything, you have to come right when dealing with him. Because it doesn't matter what you think. You need to prove it or he'll destroy you." Areesa recognized why she was President of the family's firm, but the force and tension in her voice was not enough to deter her.

"I know what he has done. From the first time I meet him, there was something in those green eyes of his, that wouldn't let me trust him. And what about the way he treats Tiffoni and the way he wants to rule over everything and everybody. Think Addie, who was helping you try and find us? Who told you how Rowan died? And why didn't he ever tell you about the trust fund?"

"I don't know. Those things weren't important at the time."

"It's important Addie," Areesa said with contempt in her voice. "I have to go. I'll call before I leave Denver. Aunt Addie, I'm sorry . . . thanks for everything you've done for me. I know you disagree with me, but I know you're still on my side."

"Someone else needs to hear that too."

"Not now, maybe even never. I'm not sure I'm the one who can give him what he wants. You know, marriage, kids, a family. I'm not sure I'm the one. I've learned a lot and I know, now, it's a lot more to love than just feeling it. Love needs taken care of, and right now I don't know if I'm capable of giving that and besides, he needs to know if it's love or pity he feels for me. I'll talk to you tomorrow."

ENTER THE WHIRLWIND

She left her room and headed for the Amethyst. She followed Tiffoni's directions, which took her in the same direction as Addie's home. The sun was beginning its decent behind the Rocky Mountains as she drove through the tree filled scenic area, about two miles or so pass Addie's gated community. The sky was streaked with hues of orange and scarlet pressing down on the blue day. Areesa turned onto the driveway and drove about one-fourth of a mile. She came to a small brick guardhouse. A middle-aged man at the gated entrance stepped out of his booth and asked for her name and who she was visiting. She waited patiently while he checked his log.

"Have a good evening Ms. Davis," he said as he opened the black steal gate for her to enter. She could see some of the estates off in the distance outlined by track lights on manicured lawns, and pathways. Flat round lollipop street lights lined the brown cobble stoned streets. The lights illuminated a soft glow into the evening night. Unlike Addie's community, these stunning houses were situated on each side of the street separated by one and a half to almost two acres of flat land and rolling hillsides. A tall brownish brick wall greeted her, appearing to be an island of its own. On it hung a sign with beautiful bronze script letters that read: Welcome to Cobblestone. From this point, vehicles had to drive to the left or right of it. She drove to the left and in the center of the street; she encountered an Old English Street lamp with directional signs on it. Each arrowed sign was imprinted with the name of each estate within the community. Amethyst's sign was pointing northwest of the entrance.

She drove towards Amethyst, the fourth estate on her left. She turned onto a thoroughfare leading to an encircled driveway enclosed by a courtyard, which extend all the way around to the brick steps leading to the front door. The stunning estate had English gardens and a raised black Brussels patio surrounded by several roman Pisa planters to the left and right of the entrance. The raven pisa border enclosed the gardens all the way around the estate. Areesa drove up slowly turning slightly to her left, as Tiffoni directed. She drove onto a second driveway that lit up with track lights from the weight of her car. Spotlights around the six-car garage came on once she stopped her car. A tall slender sable man came out of a side door to greet her. He pointed her towards a porch on the side of the house after asking for her keys.

"I can park your car in the garage, or at the front entrance."

"Thanks. Please park it at the front entrance." Amethyst, a strikingly stunning red-bricked country estate with white trim bay windows was elegantly perched among the picturesque woodlands. Instead of going in the door near her car, curiosity made Areesa follow a pathway leading to the front entrance, she wanted a better look. The sidewalk ended, and she stood looking up at a twenty foot high arched entrance and a lacquered twelve foot high side by side maple door with shinny gold sloping handles.

Once inside Areesa waited in an open foyer with sweeping grand stairs in the center of it. From where Areesa stood, she could see the sunken living room and a dimly lit study. All of the other over sized French doors were closed. Tiffoni came from under the stairs, greeting her, while jumping around chanting her name. "Areesa! Areesa you are here, I can't believe you are actually here at Amethyst!" They hugged and laughed. "Areesa I'm so glad you are here," she said again grabbing her hand and then pulling her through the spacious opulent foyer.

Areesa took it all in, feeling awkward about whether she would, or could ever be a part of Amethyst. Tiffoni whispered to her, "My Dad is home, but he hasn't mentioned his promotion ceremony." She held Areesa's hand, as she led her back beyond the sweeping stairs, bypassing the kitchen into the family room. The familyroom was arrayed with ginger colored contemporary furnishings, and fabric wallpaper imprinted with black and crimson hues, giving the room a cozy sophisticated appearance. The lighting in the room, four dropped lights from the ceiling, added a warm radiance. The room's focal points, an entertainment centered and a see-through fireplace completed the ecliptic room. "Areesa! Get in here and rescue me," she said entering the room.

The General was sitting at a counter. He was dressed in relaxed slacks and a brown long sleeve crewneck. Her mother sat on the sofa, casually dressed in a teal oversized shirt and matching pants.

"Tiffoni are you going to take her coat?"

"Oh yes, give it to me. I mean, Areesa may I take your coat?" Tiffoni hands were outstretched, and Areesa laid it across one of her arms. Tiffoni turned and neatly placed it across the back of a counter stool. "I'm so happy to see you, that I've forgotten my manners! please forgive me Areesa," she said laughing as she introduced Areesa to her Mother. The General remembered her and was delighted to have her in their home. Tiffoni asked Areesa if she wanted a drink before they began their late dinner. Areesa nodded her head up and down.

"Private Davis." She turned to face him before receiving her drink.

"Please Sir, call me Areesa."

"Ok. You look very different out of uniform, I wasn't sure if you were the same young lady," he teased.

"Areesa you do look beautiful," Tiffoni complemented. Tiffoni's Mother excused herself to check on dinner, leaving the three of them to talk about the military, because she knew that was the next direction of the conversation, if the General had his way. Tiffoni filled her own glass again. As she handed Areesa her class she quietly said, "I guess seeing Patterson agreed with you."

"No whispering you two."

"Father," Tiffoni said, without turning to face him, but searching Areesa's eyes waiting for a response. Areesa intently starred back at Tiffoni, her Buddy, her cousin knowing after she left their house, nothing would ever be the same between them. Areesa turned away, to face a wall covered by family portraits going back three, maybe four generations. She searched the wall for Rowan. Like a sore thumb, there he was, her father. She wondered if she looked like him and if she did, would either of them notice. Could the General see who she was? Tiffoni turned to see what Areesa was looking at. The General came over to the bar to fill his glass with water. "Areesa, meet the rest of our family," the General proudly stated. "I see you've taken notice of someone." Areesa dropped her head. "Don't feel embarrassed every person who has sat in this room has asked questions about the portrait that stands out to them," he informed her. "So who's your favorite?" he concluded. With her back to him, purposely not wanting to face him, her words were barely audible, "Not yet," she said starring at the track lights that shun down on the portraits giving each one a dreamlike glow.

All of the portraits surrounded a photo of a slender young woman with high check bones beneath bronze colored skin, who was flaunting the smile passed on to Tiffoni. It was their grandmother, sitting poised on an ivory Victorian chair, overshadowed by a tall chocolate man with black wavy hair and a thick mustache. Tiffoni's depiction was equally beautiful, as she sat on a settee with her legs crossed at her ankles and her hands, folded, resting on her lap, but she wasn't smiling like she normally does. Also on the wall was a family portrait of Tiffoni, her Mom, and brother with the General standing behind them in his uniform.

"Well Sir, since you've asked. Who is that man?" The General cleared his throat.

"Of all the portraits up there you're the first to ask about that one."

"Well maybe he's due his time."

"What an unusually comment for you to make"

"You're right. But still, don't you think each person deserves to have their story told?"

"I think that there are many different characters there for you to choose from besides that one."

"Why Sir, do you have something to hide about him?"

"Why would you assume such a thing?"

"Sir, we should never assume anything. Surely you know what that does."

"You are clever and engaging young lady."

"I inherited them both. Sir," she said as she turned to face him. Tiffoni came over and stood next to her. She was enjoying Areesa's word play with her Father. Areesa was challenging her Father, and she liked it. Like Tiffoni, she wasn't interested in fitting the expectations of the straight and narrow path anymore.

"Well, it seems you're not going to bore Areesa with that ancient wall."

"It appears you're right. To say the least, this young lady has made talking about our family thrilling. She's interested in your Uncle Rowan. Why do you suppose that is?"

"I haven't a clue Father. Maybe you should ask her," Tiffoni said smiling then sipping her drink. Areesa could feel his eyes watching her. Tiffoni asked if she wanted another drink, but Areesa declined. After placing his glass on the counter, the General came from behind the bar and stood between them. He moved closer to the wall after Areesa did, as Tiffoni watched them. He looked at her as she sipped what was left of her drink, and she never took her eyes off the wall. Areesa held her glass up to toast, speaking softly, so that only the General could hear her, "To the forgotten man on the wall," Areesa said. She took a sip, while peering over the rim of the glass, holding her Uncle's face in her eyes. The General bowed his head acknowledging her words. Tiffoni came up beside them and stared at each of them. The General walked away. "Areesa you've really caught my Father off guard by talking about my Uncle Rowan."

"Why?"

"He normally says Uncle Rowan isn't worth talking about because he was useless. . . not worth his breath."

"Are you sure?" Areesa asked looking at the portrait.

"What a bizarre thing for you to say Areesa."

"Why?"

"What's up with you? You're acting as obsessed about that picture as my Father does."

"Maybe we have reason to, Tiffoni. Let's ask your father," she said tracing the rim of her glass with her index finger. Areesa felt like the calm in the middle of the storm. The General's reaction confirmed all of her suspicions. She thought about what Addie said about the General's hard demeanor, but he didn't seem so hard standing next to her, looking at his past.

"Sir, Tiffoni says you, and I, are obsessed with this portrait. Do you agree?"

"My daughter unfortunately doesn't appreciate the past like she should."

"And she should, seeing how the past has left her with such a large inheritance. Let's see, how did you say it Tiffoni . . ."

"Areesa!" Tiffoni exclaimed.

"A million to the first born grandchild of the family?" Areesa finished off her drink. Without facing Tiffoni, the General calmly asked her to leave him and Areesa alone. Tiffoni hesitated, but her Father's intimidating look told her not to argue, but do as he said. As she left the room, she looked at Areesa, confused and hurt. She was usually the one causing the up roar, but for now, it was Areesa's turn. Areesa paced up and down the wall. With each step becoming more infuriated with the infallible General still giving orders. If everyone knew who and what he really was, she wondered how much authority would he have? She stopped her pacing in front of Rowan's portrait, the man who helped to create her.

"This is, what's the word ... fortuitous. The two of us obsessed with a man I've never meet, but you knew all of his life. Would you like to talk about him," she said glancing over her shoulder.

"Seeing that you're intent on talking about him, lets. He was my younger brother. Wild, wasteful and frivolous with everything he had."

"Is that why you did what you did? To keep him from getting the trust fund?"

"What do you think you know Areesa?"

"Enough. The only thing that had me goin' was why. It wasn't until we stood at this wall did it come to me. I must admit, though, at first I thought it was all about the trust fund, but after meeting you, I see. You've always had everything. The family blessing to lead them, the position as head of the Firm, the money, status, and let's not forget the all important ability to look right, without having to be right. But, last night, yea …Tiffoni's comments last night … about my Mom. She loved everyone, except you . . . at least not the way you wanted her to." The General stood as motionless as an arctic wintery night.

"You and my daughter's conversations make little sense to me. What I'd like to know, is why are you concerned about the life of a man with a soul so easily corruptible? Yes, everyone who knows this family knows my young brother was an embarrassment to all of us. And yes, there are parts of our relationship that was, strained, not as good as it should have been. But, then you also know brothers will be brothers. Other than that, what is it that you think you know?" he said looking again at Rowan's portrait. Then, unexpectedly visions of Ginny flashed before him. Memories of her flooded his thoughts, leaving him overwhelmed with her presence, as he watched his brother's physical appearance descend from the wall and envelope Areesa. "Oh, don't look so surprise General, or may I call you Uncle Robert? Yea, it's me. Rowan's get-rich-quick child, and Virginia's rising star." Her words immobilized him. "Ariisa Stryker. You don't mind if I use Stryker do you?" he uttered no words, at his brother's child standing before him. "Oh, is that all you got, where's the roar? Hey, quiet-is-kept, my father gave me a proud name. You remember him, Charlie Meaks. Davis is the name we used after he, and my mother fled Denver, like scared animals. Then again, you knew that. You know Uncle Robert," she paused, "it took me only one day to put it all together, but once I got into it the answers just fell in my lap. Imagine that?"

"I don't know what kind of hoax you're trying to pull here, but it's not going to work."

"Is that the best you can do, Uncle Robert? You know I was warned about you. That you're not to be messed with. Not a person to handle any ol' kinda way," she said mocking his response. "What is it, the past is knocking at your door too soon?" she concluded looking at him, waiting for him to strike her down and everything she was implying. But he didn't. Knowing someone else knew, his awful secret, gave him up. "Amazing, for over twenty years, you managed to conceal your betrayal against your own brother."

"Tiffoni adores you, young lady."

"I know that. And it doesn't change what you have done."

"Timing. Timing is everything. Why do you think you two ended up in the same basic training cycle?" Areesa didn't respond. He starred into her eyes. He walked up to her. Her heart punched against her chest. "You're nervous, but don't be. What did you think, when you first meet me?"

"What difference does it make?"

"It makes a difference."

"I felt honored, privilege, and I felt sad for Tiffoni. I watched her trying not to cry when you left, and I wondered how could a man so powerful, trained to fight wars and lead, not see his daughter's disappointment."

"Ouch."

"No, General . . . why?"

"You come into my home, pretending to be a friend. It is hard to fathom why you are doing this to Tiffoni. Again. Why do you think you two ended up in the same basic training cycle?"

"I don't know, destiny. Destiny," she said wondering were he was going with his question.

"Yes, destiny. Do you think we have control over destiny?"

"Yes," she paused, "Yes I do," she restated with confidence.

"You are wrong. If that is the case, then our circumstances define us. Let me give you an example. A woman dies giving birth to her daughter, who lives beyond her mother's years on this earth. The daughter becomes pregnant for the first time, and becomes paralyzed with fear that she could also die giving birth. I mean why not, if it could happen to her mother, it could happen to her. So, out of fear, she, the daughter has an abortion. Was it her child's destiny to die?" Areesa attempted to speak, but his voice overpowered hers. "Of course not, the daughter allowed her fear to dictate her destiny, to become a mother. So what should she have done? I'll tell you. She should have taken control of her circumstances, with an understanding that situations, good or bad, especially bad, can be controlled, directed if you're not afraid. What you are failing to understand is circumstances do not determine your destiny, fear does."

"Is that what you did, took control of your circumstances?"

"You and Tiffoni meeting, this situation we are discussing, is just another example of how destiny can be controlled. But I'm not afraid to control it. It is obvious you want the trust fund. Take it you can have it. You see the circumstance has been resolved" he smugly said.

"I'm not afraid either, and that's why I'm here, I want to know what happened?"

"Ok. We were young, still in high school, I enjoyed knowing Virginia," he said arrogantly with contempt in his voice. "I'll admit it, I loved her, for a moment, and for what it's worth, much more than Rowan or Charlie. It's not that she rejected me, I rejected her for not seeing the difference between my brother and I. She would tell me, Rowan and I were just alike, I was just afraid to show it."

"And you're not afraid of anything."

"No. You've heard the cliché, the only thing to fear, is fear its self."

"You make her sound like something to be had …"

"I found out she was pregnant, she was just like all the other girls living in the Lower End. Get out by getting pregnant by one of us, a *wanna-be*. That's what they called us *wanna-bes*, when all the time it was them wanting to be like us. I actually expected more from her, and yes, the situation infuriated me. I approached Rowan about her and in the heat of our argument I revealed the trust fund."

"Knowing about the trust fund is what changed his mind about wanting me? The idea of having more money is what made him want me?" she somberly asked.

"The money. Yes, the money." He laughed out loud. "Don't tell me you thought he cared, wanted you. It was the love of money, fueling his fatherly desires. Doing the honorable act of marrying her, was never a consideration. Didn't matter if he knew she loved him. How's that for circumstances."

"But my Aunt Addie said …"

"Addie? You've done your homework."

"She said Rowan cared he just didn't know how to show it."

"Now *you* sound like you want destiny to be other than what it is. Why? So you can have the fairytale. Well, you're not going to get it. You come into my home with accusations, and you want me to change your destiny," he said turning and walking away from her.

"Stop! You're a liar," she said shaking her head side to side. He turned to face her.

"The night Rowan died, I watched him and Charlie arguing, then scuffle outside, in front of a neighborhood club Charlie lived near. After I saw Charlie hit him on the head and drag his unconscious body into the alley behind the club, well …."

"You looked at your circumstances, and decided to change my dad's, and my destiny."

"No. I changed my destiny. My brother moaned he was trying to get up. At first I was going to help him, again. I watched him struggle to get up. I remember getting frustrated at his weakness … to just get up and dust himself off," the General turned to his brother's portrait, "he sat up and said 'I'm going to have him taken out as soon as I get my money. That whore did the wrong thing sending that punk after me' he said, still sitting on the ground, unwilling to . . . to be . . . I hated that more than anything, that he didn't stand for nothing. Yes, I hated him for being weak, and for always coming out on top. He swindled and destroyed everything he touched. And she, some how no longer seemed innocent to me. She was a fool like all the others for loving him, thinking some good could ever come from him."

"So what does that say about you, a man of your position and caliber? You murdered him."

"What I did is took control of my destiny."

"Listen to you, do you think what you did was right, justified!"

"I was surprised when I received it, and so was everyone else," he said ignoring her accusation, "... my commission, and I had to make sure that day didn't follow me. So, I used my family name to encourage the police to seek Charlie for questioning. I had no idea he would run. Which was fine. You see, once they did, I knew they'd never take a chance and come back."

"And you never looked back."

"No, I didn't. No one was asking me questions, and when I sat alone unable to feel sure I knew this, Virginia's love for you, and Charlie's pathetic self righteous sense of heroism would keep her, all of you away from Denver, and the truth forever. The results, Tiffoni would inherit the trust fund and I could move on with my life, and the family's good name would be secured."

"And your broken heart would be compensated because your frivolous brother was dead and you would never have to see my mother again. She did as you thought, she imprisoned herself, confined herself to guilt and sadness, that was unbearable for her. She was so beautiful. She gave so much of herself to everyone, even you probably, it just wasn't the way you wanted it. You had to control her. You and your brother are just alike. Selfish. I think I can speak for her in saying, it is a sad thing what you've done. Your so-called way of expressing destiny, is an illusion, you have bought into all of our lives, especially your own. What's going to become of everyone who loves you and depend on your honor?" The General turned to face his family on the wall. He walked away from the wall, and took a seat. He sat calmly, blank faced in his leather over stuffed chair near the fireplace. "What you plan to do, is all that matters now, would you not agree?" Areesa looked down on the broken man and felt pity for him as she made her intentions clear.

"I do want my inheritance. It's rightfully mine. I'll let you tell Tiffoni, your lovely wife and son, because I can't face Tiffoni with what I know about the man I know she loves very much. As for everything else, I haven't decided what to do. Maybe somewhere in your heart you'll feel compelled to free my parents and do the right thing by the two, no the three of them." Areesa turned and faced the man who helped to create her, then she turned and faced the man who nearly destroyed her. They were so much alike. It astounded her that the

General didn't see how much alike he and his brother were. She walked to the double French doors, and slowly pulled them open with both of her hands. She walked back the way Tiffoni had lead her. Tiffoni was sitting on the beautiful stairs, her moisten face told Areesa she heard some of, if not most of what went on. They looked at each other. Areesa smiled at her Buddy, then turned to put on her coat. Tiffoni stood up on the bottom stair, she didn't say anything and neither did Areesa. As she looked at Tiffoni, she was reminded of how graceful she could be when she wanted to. Tiffoni, tried to smile as she lifted her right hand up and waved. Areesa waved back and smiled. She hoped someday she and Tiffoni could build a true relationship without their fathers' trespasses against each other, lingering over them.

Areesa turned grabbed hold of the brass handles of the beautiful maple wood door and pulled them down releasing the doors to swing open. The cold evening air caressed her face as she walked under the threshold into the night. She was free and her parents' honor was restored.

The next day she went to see Addie. She filled Addie in on everything that happened and Addie was amazed and heartbroken by the events that had taken place. She was also able to regain her freedom from the past and the guilt she felt from the roll she played. They planned to meet in New Jersey after Areesa finished her Advance Training, so the two of them could visit her parents' graves and share memories of them.

"The siege has ceased, and peace is at hand. Now I can move forward with my life."

"Are you going to get in touch with Antonis?" Addie asked

"No."

Areesa and Addie spent that evening together. Areesa left the next morning to check out of her room. She checked out early, paid for the broken items in her room and extended her rental car contact for a drop at the airport. As she was leaving, she asked the clerk for directions to the mall. Her bags were loaded into her car and she spent her remaining hours in Denver, exploring. She felt comfortable doing things in Denver. The city had become her city, too. After shopping at the Cherry Creek Mall, she headed for the airport. She turned the car in and headed for the terminal. As the phones came into view, she stared at them, wanting one to get up and reposition its self in front of her, making it easy for her to call him, but she passed them by resisting the temptation to call him. They were together for a season and that season had passed. What they were supposed to do in each other's life was done and now it was time for them to go their separate ways. Areesa walked through the security area without beeping. She waited for her purse and carry on bag to go through the x-ray. She picked her things up and continued her leisurely walk to the shuttle train. The doors slid open and she took her seat. She watched the train maneuver through the tunnel. She got off and went up the escalator to her gate. Along the way she stopped at an eatery, purchased a bottled water and sandwich to eat while she waited to board her plane. She rode the escalator and fumbled with her bags to get them to hang on her body more comfortably. She made her way through the airport to the sitting area where a few people were already waiting. The weight of her bags hanging from her shoulders, strained her body, so she freed her body by letting the bags slip from her shoulders into an empty chair. She sat down, and then placed her food on top of her things in the chair to her right. She lifted her bottom, so that she could pull the discarded newspaper from under her. The front cover of the paper took her breath way. It read: U.S. Army General Robert Stryker Commits Suicide.

no more running

Areesa finished her military Advance Individual Training (AIT) in the top five percent of her class. AIT was not as lonely as Basic Training. She received letters and care packages from Addie, and when graduation came, Addie was out in the massive crowd calling her name, and waving at her. After her graduation, she and Addie flew to New Jersey, to visit her parents' graves. It was a time of grieving and forgiving, as they said their good-byes to them. The two shared stories about her parents. Each story blessing their lives and relationship in a way neither of them expected.

During their stay in Jersey, Addie arranged for a leasing company to manage Virginia and Charles' house, because Areesa wouldn't consider selling it, and Addie agreed. Addie also pulled a few strings that made it possible for Areesa to get a duty assignment at the Fort in Colorado so they could be close in distance.

Addie remained President of Stryker Financial Firm after the General's suicide, while Gramps, gladly, came out of retirement to step in as CEO. Areesa didn't go to the General's memorial service, but she did send her condolence to Tiffoni via a letter briefly expressing her feelings about what happened and she encouraged Tiffoni to remain strong, because she knew how it felt to lose a parent. Tiffoni welcomed and received her letter and wrote her back openly extending an invitation to visit Gramps and the rest of the family. Areesa graciously accepted. Soon after the funeral, Tiffoni received a hardship discharge from the army, and took up the position as Head of the Family, without becoming CEO. She openly confessed it would tie her down to the point that she couldn't breathe. Her position was clear to everyone, when she wanted to go, she was going. Addie kept Areesa up to date on Tiffoni's antics, "The child gives her mother an allowance, and tells her that at some point she needs to earn her own income."

"In other words, get a job mom," Areesa said laughing, and Addie agreed.

"She is constantly demanding that her brother stop shamming as an Army Officer, come home, and become the CEO. Other than that she is handling things well," Addie said teasingly.

"Still Tiffoni, which is all good."

In the face of her father's suicide, that left her momentarily wounded, Tiffoni was going on with her life. Living not on her father's coattail of success, but on her own success.

Areesa and Tiffoni split the inheritance, which made it easy for both of them. Areesa girlishly admitted she didn't know what to do with all that money. So, at her request Addie immediately and cheerfully used the firm's legal staff to arrange for the release of the inheritance into their private accounts. "I'm so very proud of you girls. This is the right thing to do," Addie praised.

THREE ½ YEARS LATER …

The connection between Areesa, Addie, and Tiffoni became unbreakable. Areesa was living her life free of her parents' decisions, Addie made peace with the past, and Tiffoni was rebuilding her family's legacy to one of honor. The three established a full-scholarship to a four year college or university for a high school senior who was the firstborn in their family, which would allow him or her to select what college they wanted to attend. They held an annual community block party in the Lower End to raise money and awareness of organizations that supported young unwed mothers and the importance of service.

Areesa made the rank of Sergeant. With Addie and Tiffoni's encouragement, love, and advice, she made a life changing decision about her future in the army as she was nearing the end of her four-year enlistment obligation. She decided not to re-enlist. With her Bachelor Degree in communication, she felt confident about taking on a new career in broadcasting or public relations. Besides, the Army had done its part in her life and it was time for her to move on. She was stable, and rooted in an abundance of security and self-understanding. She didn't think she would overcome the lost of her parents, because of the way things unraveled, but she did. It was time for her to move on to the next chapter of her life. Once her decision was made, Addie and Tiffoni were constantly pushing her to join the firm, but she declined. She explained she felt like a smorgasbord of everyone in her life, so, for that reason the firm would not be the place for her. Everything in her life had come together, solidified by her financial freedom. As she made left, right, and wrong turns she held dear to her heart Tiffoni's words from what seemed like an eternity ago: Know who you are, because money changes people, especially when they don't recognize they have money, it doesn't have them. Areesa learned Tiffoni's only exception to that philosophy.

"Areesa, when one is shopping, you have to flip the switch, because this is the time when money has you."

"You know I can really learn to enjoy this shopping thing."

"After shopping we can go to dinner. Hey call your Auntie and ask if she'd like to join us."

"I'm not going to tell her we are shopping again, she'll be too through with both of us."

"I know. For all the shopping we do she thinks we need …"

"A fella," they both said laughing hysterically.

"She cracks me up when she says it like that, a fell-uh. Besides you already have a fella." Areesa stopped laughing. "I know you don't talk about him, but do you ever think about him Areesa?"

"If my life hadn't been turned upside down like it was, he wouldn't have ever shown me the attention he did. So, no. Not really." Tiffoni and Addie thought other wise.

"It's ok if you do. Why is it so hard for you to admit that you think of him?" Without waiting for her to respond, she went on, "If it was me I would, a lot. For that matter I would wonder if I would ever see him again."

"That's why you are you, and I'm me." Without acknowledging her, Tiffoni walked over to a store window. Areesa followed her, "With all my hang ups and issues, I'm not sure if he cared about me or felt sorry for me."

"Oh that's cute, let's go in. Areesa we all have hang ups, issues. And if we waited until they were all satisfied, recognized, realized, put aside, and, or justified before we loved someone the world would be a place without love."

"So what do you suggest I do."

"Not what you doin'."

"Ok, that's not an answer."

"Well, only God himself knows that answer. In the mean time you need to stop acting like he doesn't exist. Like he just went poof, back to Drill Sergeant land."

"That's easy for you to say Tiffoni." Tiffoni looked through the rack at the beautiful dresses for her size. She stopped and turned to face Areesa. "You know people make loving each other so difficult, when all it's really about is spending time together in some store. Talking about everything and nothing, or moving a sofa from one end of the house to the other, knowing each other is all right. When you see your Bho coming you should smile on the inside because the two of you know you are loving each other the way only the two of you can love each other. And I'll tell you something else Areesa, sitting outside on the porch on a beautiful day talking and laughing with family and friends, is what makes love, love. Not weather you have issues beyond your control."

"My Auntie Addie told you that didn't she?" There was ten seconds of silence.

"Yea, she did. The porch gave me away, didn't it? I should have said garden," they both began laughing, "but did I get it right?"

"Yea, Buddy, you got it right."

. . . KEEPING IT MOVIN'

"A new day, hour, minute to live a good life," she repeated to herself over and over as she ran through the streets of her fort at 0-6-hundred hours. On this morning, she allowed herself to remember him. Letting her mind run away with thoughts of him lead her to their park. She stopped running once she reached the place where they parked, and talked about everything and nothing. For the first time in three years, after driving by it at least twice a week without ever stopping, she stood where they stood, and longed for him. She walked the same path they did, and stopped at the same spots they did so long ago. She touched the two large trees they stood between when he told her he loved her. She sat at the table under the oak near the stream, like they did. Sitting there, she wondered if he ever thought of her, as she remembered how he held her in his arms, and she remembered the weight of his body when he encircled her in his arms. She inhaled, and remembered his scent and felt his gentle hands caressing her face. She closed her eyes, imagining him there with her. She wanted to sit with her eyes closed forever, so he could be with her. Never wanting to talk about him was easier, than talking about him. "How do you talk about what you'll never have? My heart aches for you Sergeant Antonis Patterson," she said dropping her head, smiling, remembering how caring and giving he was with her, even when she didn't know his name. Now she knows his name, and he's not with her. She laughed, quietly, and sadly, because she was certain she could never love anyone the way she realized she loved him. She sighed. "Time to go. It is what it is, and it's time to say good-bye," she said standing, then looking around the park, feeling a sense of contentment in knowing she had achieved what he wanted most for her, happiness. And she was happy with her life.

. . . LATER THAT DAY

Warm weather on a calm serene sunshine day, with a blue sky filled with popcorn like clouds sitting on top of gigantic mountain peaks, and lush green surroundings around the fort and throughout the city of Colorado Springs, was breathe taking as she walked across the lawn from another building back to her office.

Areesa was assigned to the Post Public Affairs Office. She was in her office preparing to go home when two, of her three soldiers came in to update her on the status of a few pending documents. After releasing her last soldier for the day, she packed up her backpack, and did her routine closing and security check of the office. First, she made sure office details were done by checking her soldiers' detail list: Empty trashcans, clean latrine, turn off equipment. She went over the duty list to make sure all office correspondence and suspense-dated memos had been completed. As she secured the safe, she noticed that her only female soldier, a Specialist who was preparing for the Promotion Board, left her study guide. Areesa picked it up and put it in her backpack so she could give it to her at some point over the weekend. She gathered the rest of things, and checked all doors, making sure they were locked. She turned off the lights, and left her office, looking forward to a peace and quiet weekend.

Areesa lived in the Mountainside Condominium Complex close enough to the fort that she could walk the half-mile home on sunny days. After jiggling the doorknob, she paused a moment to absorb the evening air. She looked down at the ground and made a nasty face, then picked up the "BUTT" can and moved it to the side of her building. She still hated the habit. She brushed her hand a couple of times against her thigh to get the soot off as she began her walk home, making a mental note to do a good police walk for trash Monday morning. Her Sergeant Major was leaving the building across from her, she waved and wished him a happy weekend. He returned the gesture as he waved back at her. Sergeant First Class (SFC) Archer, who worked in the building next door walked towards her.

"What's up Sgt. Davis, or can I call you Areesa, now?"

"Sure Sergeant Archer. What's up?" she said ginning as he came closer to her.

"I'm having a Bar-b-Que at my place. A few friends, plenty of good food, and loud music. I was hoping you might stop by, get yourself a plate, maybe stay a minute, or two. I promise you'll have a good time," he said smiling down at her.

"Well … I don't know. You see I got my backpack and it's filled with work. So I don't know."

"Aw, come on Davis. Ok, ok. I tell you what, I'm on the roster, give me a call if you change your mind," he said disappointedly.

"Thanks for the invite, I do appreciate it, but I …"

"Come on Baby-girl, all you do is work! You gotta enjoy life sometimes. Every time I see you, you …" As he continued his effort to convince her to hangout with him, she starred intently into his face watching every facial expression, movement of his lips, flicker in his eyes. Her eyes watched his mouth move as she thought about what a nice guy he is, but she wasn't feeling his vibe, a connection, any feeling advising her that she should spend one-on-one time with him. She had tried a couple of times to date seriously, but the two guys she did give a chance couldn't hang with her expectations. Unknowing to them, she was measuring each man up to the image of a man they had never seen or talked to. "It's hard trying to fit into Superman's suit," one of them eventually told her about her expectations of him. She laughed.

"What's so funny?" he asked.

"Oh, nothing. Hey thanks for the invite, but I'm sure I won't be able to make it. Maybe some other time." She knew eventually the relationship would end, like the other two because she understood from past experience, and talking to him she wasn't going to get what she needed to make her feel the way she wanted, safe, adored, and *lovely*.

A car stopped, on the other side of the street, in front of them. It was Areesa's female soldier. Sergeant Archer said good-bye as her soldier approached them holding her head down. She knew Areesa was going to get on her for forgetting her study material. Areesa held up the study guide, and waved it in the air. She intended to drop her, but the Specialist's effort to come back, was worth something, so she didn't. She handed her the study guide, fussed a little, and then wished her a good weekend.

Areesa walked out of the fort's front gate towards a fruit and vegetable stand a couple of blocks down the street. She stopped to purchase strawberries, kiwi, bananas, green apples and a bundle of fresh flowers. The attendant saw her at least once a week since the weather turned warm, and he enjoyed seeing her. He noticed much about her, especially how attractive she was in her BDU uniform and spit shined boots. He also noticed, there was a sadness about her, in spite her effort to hide behind her smile and beautiful bright eyes.

"Have a lovely evening Sergeant Davis," he said giving her her change, fruit, and flowers wrapped in cellophane.

"You too," she said. What a sweet man she thought as she headed towards her condo.

... A HALF OF MILE LATER

Once inside her condo, Areesa unpacked her backpack, and then put her flowers in water. She sat on her sofa and scanned through her mail, as she took off her boots and sweaty uniform shirt. "Ooo, I'm so glad to be home," she said standing to loosen her belt buckle as she headed for the refrigerator.

She took out a package of meat, grabbed a bottled water, then walked back into her living room. She checked her messages as she took off her socks and t-shirt.

Message one:

"Areesa are you coming up for the weekend, let me know. If not I guess I could drive down, but you know how me and the army get along. We don't. Give me a buzz as soon as you get in. Hey, Gramps wants . . ." BEEP.

"You only get forty-five seconds Tiffoni," she said to the machine.

Message two:

"Hi Sweetie how are you? Just calling to see if you're coming up. Give me a call when you can. Love ya." BEEP

Message three:

"Sergeant Davis I forgot my study book. Can I stop by and get the keys to the office? Give me a call. Thanks. Oh . . . its Specialist McNeil." BEEP

Areesa listened to the machine reset, then she went into the bathroom to take a shower. After her shower, she cooked her meal and sat down on the sofa to enjoy it as she watched TV.

Her condominium was open and spacious. She loved being at home. The kitchen was small, but well equipped with a microwave, garbage disposal, dishwasher, and side-by-side refrigerator with an icemaker, and beautiful oak cabinets and black granite counters. Her house was decorated with big green lush plants that filled the wall ledges and alcoves, and earthy brown, orange, light auburn, and green colored furnishing, pillows were everywhere, and scented by white linen candles. Tiffoni said her house was too cozy and romantic to be without a fella. Areesa laughed because she knew Tiffoni was once again trying to provoke her in to admitting she was lonely. "I'm alone Tiffoni, not lonely," she admitted.

"Yea, yea. Yadda, yadda. Semantics," Tiffoni would respond.

Before she became too comfortable, she returned Tiffoni and Addie's calls to let them know she was driving up on Saturday. Of course, Tiffoni wanted to know why tomorrow. Exasperated by her determination to get her up there before she wanted, Areesa told her she had work from the office she wanted to get done first. Only then did Tiffoni let up. She hung up the cordless phone and headed towards her favorite chill-out spot in her condo.

During the summer, Areesa unwind on her balcony that faced Pikes Peak in Antonis' park. She enjoyed sitting outside sipping her favorite drink, watching the sunset. She put the phone down on a table, sat down on a cloth-covered patio lounge chair, and rested her head on its back waiting for the sun to set. She closed her eyes for a moment, and enjoyed the evening breeze as it blew softly across her face. As the sun began its decent, the sky turned crimson orange, a perfect backdrop for the Rockies. Always different, and better than the one before. "Beautiful, just beautiful," she said. Suddenly, a familiar sense of loneliness came over her, but she shook it off and immediately used one of her effective tools to fight the feeling, work.

As the night grew darker, she turned on the shaded lamp on the centered of the table she was working on. As time crept by she couldn't take it anymore-the large illuminated Baskin & Robin Ice Cream marquee gleaming like a guiding light. The ice cream polar was located at a strip mall about a block from her house. Before it got any darker, she was up getting her keys heading for the door to walk across the street to get ice cream.

"Mmm, yummy for my tummy, Very Berry Strawberry here I come," she said, crossing the busy street at the light.

As she walked towards the mall, she pondered what was going on with her, she'd been thinking of Antonis, more frequently than ever before. She shrugged it off, thinking it was the time in the park earlier in the day that had her going. She felt sad as she considered the reason why she didn't allow herself to remember him. She didn't want to experience what she did during basic, unable to keep him from again and again creeping into her thoughts. She hoped allowing herself this time to get swept away by the memories would calm her recurring feeling of loneliness. Yet, she was struggling to shut the memories down, especially the time he said he loved her. The only difference in that moment of time is she told him she loved him too and they lived happily ever after. But that dream was always taken over by that night on Addie's lawn, when she told him love didn't matter. "Stop it. I can't keep reliving this. Go away," she said to her thoughts, and the memory went away as she commanded.

She walked through the cross walk at the intersection and onto the mall parking lot on the end where most of the stores where. She weaved through some vehicles, navigating her way towards Baskin & Robins on the opposite end. The closer she came towards the ice cream shop the more her mouth anticipated the cool delight. When she came to the front of an auto store Areesa came to a sudden stop. Inside the brightly lit shop was a man. Her eyes were captured by this man standing at the counter with his back to her. It didn't matter how he stood, she knew him. She gasped, and her heart fluttered. Her feet felt like cement blocks, keeping her from moving forward or backwards, left or right. The salesperson on the other side of the counter was chatting away and smiling as if he was telling a joke. As the man began to turn, she instinctively raised both of her hands to cover her mouth, as she held her breath, waiting to see the man's face. He turned, but he was looking down at his hand as he placed his money in his wallet. The store's brightly shinning light revealed his handsome face. Yet, she doubted her eyes as she watched him approach the door, "Is that really you? Antonis." Without looking up he leaned into the glass door to open it. As he walked out of the door, he looked up and immediately recognized her standing less than ten steps from him. "Antonis," her lips moved, but no sound came out as her heart leaped. Unaware of moving cars, people, the world, they moved together towards each other, without hesitation or either of them uttering a word. He came to the edge of the curb and she stepped onto the curb with only a few inches between them.

"Areesa," he whispered in disbelief. "Areesa, you're here."

"Yes. You're here."

"I know. I mean, I know, I can't believe it either."

"It's you. I can't believe this, it's you Antonis."

"Yea it's me," he said then they started laughing. She reached out and gently pressed her hand against his face. He closed his eyes, absorbing the feel of her hand. He reached out to take hold of her other hand. They lingered in the same feeling they felt that day in his office, a feeling of warmth, and genuine desire to be a part of each other for no other reason than knowing he was him and she was her. He pulled her gently into his arms and softly kissed her on her forehead. "I can't believe you are here, taking hold of my heart."

"Please forgive me," he said.

"Forgive you? I'm praying to God my eyes are not deceiving me. You're here," she said with her face snuggled against his chest.

"Naw, Bho, I should have told you what was goin' on." She sighed at the sound of his voice calling her by that name, "You're not being deceived. We're here. We're together," he said squeezing her tight.

"Shhh, I'm listening to your heart beat, so I'll never forget what it sounds like."

"Ok," he said laughing softly, remembering how sweet and innocent she was.

"How long have you been here?"

"About three weeks. When I in-processed they were in the field. First Sergeant mentioned I probably wouldn't have to go, but you know how that goes as soon as I got my TA-50 I was on my way down range."

"Oh wow. How long did you stay?"

"I didn't, I sat in the Barracks about seven days. Then they needed me some place else, but First Sergeant said if he didn't hear from them by Friday, for me not to worry about it. Bho, I was holding my breath, because God knew I didn't wanna go. They didn't call, and I hit the door. They haven't seen me since. That was about five, five-thirty." She laughed, enjoying the sound of his voice. He told her, "I've been all over this city, just riding. Checking out the mountains, looking at places to live, buying a few things and thinking about you. Wishing we where here, together again."

"Antonis, I . . ."

"You know what," he said looking into her face, she shrugged her shoulders up and down, "I don't know why I stopped at this mall. Cause check this out, the car I'm driving is a rental. My truck hasn't gotten in off the boat yet." They laughed and hugged.

"I've never stopped thinking about you Areesa. I kept asking myself why isn't she trying to get in touch with me? Knowing you it was to give me a chance to find out if my love for you was real. Real in my own heart. And yea, I did eventually want to know for myself too. I searched my feelings for you long and hard and all I kept coming back to was a lonely man desiring a woman who wouldn't accept his love."

"Antonis, I . . .," he placed his finger to her lips silencing her.

"I want and need you in my life. I love you because of you. Not the past, only the present, right here and now, is what really matters. I respect you Baby for looking out for me." Tears were flowing down her face as he passionately revealed his heart. "Bho the world is big and it's hard out there for me not knowing if you're ok, living good, not because you are better or less than anyone else, but because you deserve it. I don't want to live my life not knowing if you are well with this world."

A silence fell between them like never before. Areesa's love for him was the strongest emotions she had ever felt in her life. She knew he was the man promised to her before either of them were born. She was him and he was her, and their love was bound together long before Basic Training. She looked into his eyes, and at that moment, he entered her being, and touched her soul. Time had helped her become as sure of her love for him, as she knew the sun would rise the next day.

"Marry me? Bho, will you marry me?" he asked her knelling down to one knee right there on the curb pressing her hands against his heart, he looked up into her beautiful brown eyes. Feeling the warmth of his skin against her own, she felt as if they had never been apart, words could never define for another human being what she felt about the second chance they were getting. Mesmerized by the moment, she starred into his eyes knowing, only God knew what was intended for her, and him. As her eyes filled with tears she knew he was the man she was suppose to encounter that day in a cold building three and half years ago.

"Yes. Yes, Bho, I'll marry you."

the end

www.ingramcontent.com/pod-product-compliance
Lightning Source LLC
Chambersburg PA
CBHW052135170626
46812CB00004B/1439